I Don't
Remember You

Stephanie Lennox

A big thank you to all
my friends and the teachers at

Lambeth Academy
(2007 - 2009), for restoring
my belief in good people.

My Mum and Dad
for teaching me the values
I hold so dear today.

And to my boyfriend Sam,
for an unforgettable year.

Thank you.

Chapter 1
...When things were happy.

It was when she was five years old, that her mother predicted the future for her.

She saw a bright spark in school, someone that would grace national TV almost every day in every spelling bee and decathlon the academic system had to offer. She saw a graduation that had come about with total ease for her extremely clever daughter. She saw a successful career next that made enough money for three houses, all in tropical countries, of course, and then...dare she say it? A glorious wedding, with no trimmings spared. A handsome man who could equal her in intelligence and appearance, and be able to support the family. Three fat grandchildren, she predicted. Then it would all be perfect.

It wasn't Jasmine's fault that she wasn't the bright spark that her mother had hoped for exactly. Not to say that she wasn't intelligent because she was, but Jasmine had fainted when it was her cue to say "Baa," in the school's nativity play, so she was hardly ever likely to appear on TV. As if that wasn't bad enough, her choice of love interest was also someone who didn't fit her mother's mould. But that wasn't her fault either. Life has a strange way of panning out. Who would stop the seductive advances and the sensual touches of their lover to dwell on something their parents planned for them? Exactly. When you know, you know, and you can't change or reject the person you knew you loved in an instant...

A flicker of movement outside the kitchen window tempted her eye and she partially returned to the real world; shuddering as she observed the suburban neighbourhood she lived in, and knowing it was a world she didn't belong to. Biting her nails while she watched a group of carefree children run past, she wondered what her mother would say if she could see her now. Go ahead and laugh, mum, she thought to herself. Everything in her life seemed "wrong". She'd promised her mother that by the time she abandoned her teenage years she'd abandon the odd smelling diner she worked in, too. She wanted to cry every time she handed over the rent money for the apartment, knowing that it wasn't worth half what she was paying, and that the toilet in the back had never been in working order. And yet, why did those things seem trivial today?

Because today was March 15th.

From the alleyway outside her window, a female figure appeared right on time. Her heart jumped as soon as she saw the shadow beyond the trees, and now she had no idea whether to be excited or nervous. She wasn't afraid because of this girl, per say - she was a perfectly ordinary girl to anyone else's eye. Her mousy brown, medium length hair was unkempt as usual, and in a ponytail today. Jasmine took it as a sign that she'd been playing football which was good, hopefully it meant she'd be more relaxed. She had cold but sparkly blue eyes that could pierce into anyone's soul, and freckles around her nose that she always complained about. Slim and athletically built, she could easily pull off wearing the denim shorts and a light blue top that she had on anytime. She was a funny, confident girl - and her name was Becca.

"Let her in, Dad!" Jasmine called. She breathed out excitedly, brushed her hair out of her face and lifted a big silver box out from under the sink and adjusted the pink ribbon on the top so it was perfectly straight. It wasn't even her birthday, but she was sure she was going to burst with all the excitement. She'd secretly obsessed over this day for weeks, taking so much joy in finding exceptional new ways to make it special. She'd scoured the internet each night trying to find the most perfect, unique present, but nothing had felt quite right - until eventually she peeked into the old forgotten wardrobe in her mother's room and there it was.

"Come on then! Let's get this over with!" Someone shouted from the sitting room. Jasmine let out a laugh, more like a splutter, and was glad Becca wasn't in the room to witness how nervous she was.

Since she'd been thinking about her mother all morning, she'd realised how little she talked to her, "upstairs", and made a silent vow that she would make an effort to do so more from now on. *Hey Mum*, she thought loudly in her head. *Sorry we haven't talked in a long while. I miss you. This present is something of yours, I guess you know that, but I hope you also know that it's not because I'm forgetting about you. I wouldn't be giving something of yours away to just anyone.*

She took a breath and entered her living room. In just one moment, all the fears and worries Jasmine had carried around with her all morning simply disappeared into nothing. Nothing mattered more than the here and now, with her girlfriend of two years, who was sitting in her front room and appeared just as thrilled as she was. True, she would have given anything to know what her mother thought of her relationship this morning. But now as all the feelings she had for Becca came flooding back into her senses, she realised that her mother could only smile at affection as deep as what she felt here, if she was any kind of mother at all. Jasmine compared the way she felt to someone who'd seen the sun for the first time. It was like an overwhelming sense of relief - like the balance in the world had finally been restored and everything was now finally the way it should be.

I hope you can see how amazing we are together, and that I know you only wanted the best for me...but I won't ever need a handsome man and a glorious wedding. I will only ever need her.

"Hey. Happy Birthday," She said shakily.

Becca sighed, making sure her indignation was known as she accepted the present, but Jasmine just smiled and ignored her as she opened the wrapping. She knew that for Becca, another birthday just meant a boring church service dedication courtesy of her mum, a crappy present from Harry, her brother, and another year of struggling to get out of the town on a poor man's salary. But Jasmine never let her down, and always provided her with the most elaborate of presents every year, without fail. Jasmine's smile widened when she picked out a beautiful garment of clothing from the box, then turned to her with her mouth wide open.

"Good God, Jasmine! Is this what I think it is?"

With a flick of her wrist, Becca unravelled a beautiful black coat into the lounge. It demanded attention from the room due to its regality, its gold buttons and the softest, glossiest faux fur. A piece of metal clicked through her fingers, and on closer inspection she noticed a brooch; a fruit basket, with jewelled fruit that danced before her eyes. She realised that she was standing gormless as she stared at the beautiful coat, not only because of its eye-appeal, but because she knew that it had belonged to Jasmine's mother. She looked at her as if she'd gone mad, completely dumbfounded as to how Jasmine could give away such a sentimentally valued item.

"Why would you give me this?"

"Because you always said you liked it. And, to be honest, I didn't have a lot of money to get you anything new..." She laughed.

"Don't joke. Jasmine! This is so amazing! No one's ever given me such a thoughtful thing. But your mum-"

"-Would want you to have it." She said, smiling reassuringly.

"Oh God. Thank you...so much."

Jasmine felt Becca's soft hands brush her hair out her face. She was shuffling about like a school girl again, looking as if she wanted to say something but for some reason, couldn't. It just wasn't like her to share emotions, so she tried her best to snap out of it and continued to talk like everything was normal again.

"...Well! I think I'm gonna run back to my house and change into something prettier to go with this. My football top and these shorts are hardly going to cut it, are they? Then we can go to the cinema, like you planned."

She mocked a gasp. "How did you know?"

"Every year, Jas. Every year."

Jumping over to open the door, Jasmine watched her lover put the coat on for the first time. It was a little big, and the hood looked as if it was completely swallowing her face, but all the same both of them smiled at each other goofily before Becca rushed out to complete her errands. As she watched Becca step out onto the road with it on, Jasmine felt like God had truly blessed her with knowing someone so important, and no one could have taken away the way she felt at that moment. She felt like every sense she had was wide awake: every scent, every touch and every sight was more vivid to her than ever before. She smiled to herself, and she felt as if no one would be able to take this amazing feeling away from her. Unfortunately, she was about to find out that she'd spoken too soon. Just before she turned to go inside, to finish preparing the amazing dinner she'd made for when Becca got back, she took one last glance outside.

It wasn't until Jasmine saw a shiny black car connect with the back of Becca's leg as she tried to cross, that all smiles faded. There was a terrifying moment where Jasmine couldn't breathe...and she felt as if she was in an awful nightmare. One of those where your mouth feels sore from yelling but no one can hear, and the ones where you're underwater, trying to punch and kick but you just can't seem to touch anything real. Things went into terrifying slow motion. Becca flew into the windscreen of the car- splattering blood through the broken window and onto the driver, from her now fractured cheekbones. There was a horrific splintering sound from Becca's hip and leg bone because they both had snapped, and her very lifeless looking body slid off the car, and landed in a heap on the road.

Jasmine.

It took a long time for Jasmine to realise that it was in fact <u>her</u> screams that she could hear vibrating off every window in the neighbourhood.

Why is the ground shaking beneath my feet? She wondered. *Why has the world gone into mute, all blurry and messed up?*

She fought through the shock and her crippling urge to run to the body, and dashed to her phone in the kitchen to ring the ambulance first. She'd seen too many movies to leave the phone call too long, when it's usually the thing that saves the person's life. After screaming down the phone at an inexperienced phone assistant as tears streamed down her face, she rushed back outside only to see the black car speeding off. Her heart sank to a lower place than it had ever been before as she realised she hadn't written down the license plate...but she ignored the feeling and dragged herself over to Becca's frigid body. Jasmine's father, Archie, suddenly stumbled out of the house in his dressing gown, his eyes red and sleepy at first, but then tense and horrified at the scene. Nothing could have prepared him for this. As he crept closer, his face scared Jasmine even more than the sight of the blood that was everywhere. She knew her dad was never one to panic. Archie <u>never</u> panicked. He usually made a wise crack then walked away, and never just stared blankly like the way he was doing at that moment. "Dad, what do I do?" she said quietly, trying to get him to snap out of it. "What do I do, dad?"

When he said nothing, Jasmine screamed. Her voice triggered some movement into him finally, and he leapt forward. Jasmine could see every cog in his brain start to roll. His eyes darted around as he noticed all the people pouring out of their houses, wondering what a man was doing out on the street in his dressing gown, until they saw the blood. Then the buzzing started. Delicious new gossip from a town that already hated both of them. It was almost as if Jasmine could see a demon inside every one of the people, clawing its way out of their mouths and lapping up the scent of the catastrophe from the air with their long pointy tongues. Jasmine closed her eyes in an attempt to stop the tears, and she muffled her sobs and moans into Becca's hair. She hated crowds, especially bad ones.

Archie began yelling. "We need towels! Come on, all of you! You there! Help me bring this over to block the road. If you're not going to help, then get back inside your homes and stop gawping!"

Jasmine let out a sigh of relief as people finally started to help, stirring into action just like Archie had. She hoped Becca had just stopped when it all happened, too. She hoped that Becca was mentally somewhere else now, much nicer than here. In shock, and in no pain....because the thought of Jasmine in pain almost made her throw up.

"Becca. Becca! Can you hear me? Please tell me you can hear me..."

Becca's hands and her vision was shaking, she could only see blurry pictures now. She felt like she was fading away into nothing...but then she felt warm arms around her and even though it was blurred, she recognised Jasmine. She was singing to her and her beautiful, calming voice was enough to soothe any person to sleep....and even though Becca felt like that's all she wanted to do at the moment, she stayed awake to listen.

Why was I such an idiot? She thought to herself. *I should have stayed...I should have stayed with her. It's funny how at the one time I can't talk, is the time when I have all the right words.*

It made her grind her teeth thinking about how much time she'd spent teasing and pretending to be tough, and realised now she should have spent it telling Jasmine how she really felt. She would have told her that even if this was the end, and she died, that her life would not have been half as special without her and she had loved every moment. She really wished she could tell her. Ten long, slow minutes passed, and she'd stayed awake just long enough to see some painfully bright blue and red flashing lights.

* * * *

A scream brought Becca back out of a short unconscious spell she'd been in. It was Jasmine again, and this time she was fiercely crying out for her to stay awake, to stay with her. She hated seeing Jasmine so upset, and even though she was in so much pain, she felt like Jasmine was still her biggest priority. They were in the back of the hospital van now - Becca felt an air mask around her face, and the worst, most intense burning sensations in her limbs that she'd ever felt in her life. She tried to talk but instead, a gurgling sound came up from within, and she threw up all over the seating. Then everything went black again.

* * * *

Jasmine had never felt this crap in her whole life...and with hardly any more tears to shed, she was now just staring into space, sipping a tasteless cup of instant coffee, and wishing she was in Becca's place in the hospital bed. At least then, she could be inhaling some of that sweet, sweet morphine like Becca was right now. It seemed to be working okay for her.

She sipped her coffee again slowly then looked outside to the nurses reception desk through the window. Becca's mother Gina and her brother Harry had arrived about 20 minutes ago and were still arguing to be let into Becca's hospital room...but the lovely nurse was keeping them out for a while, until they calmed down at least. Eventually the nurse sighed and came into the room, and Jasmine jumped up. She knew what was coming next, but even the thought of leaving Becca made her feel like she was dying inside. Jasmine flung herself at her feet and begged with all her might. "Please, please don't let them in yet. She's mine," Jasmine sobbed. "She's mine! And I can't leave her now, not like this. I just want to be alone with her, just for a few more minutes."

The nurse looked at her with sympathetic eyes, but her mouth opened as if she was going to say that she had to stay professional, and had to let the family in by law or something. Jasmine tried again, her voice hardly louder than a whisper. "Please...? I know they're her family, but she's everything to me. You just can't..." Before she could finish her sentence she relapsed into sobs again, having used up all her energy. Thankfully her hearty speech got the nurse herself welling up in tears, and having melted her heart, she then went dutifully to try for a few more minutes. Jasmine put her coffee down onto the floor, then scooted her chair closer to Becca. After staring at her a while with her red tear stained eyes, she leaned forward so her lips were just brushing Becca's ear, and whispered to her as softly as she could.

"My heart is only beating for you, Becca. You keep yours beating for me."

She began to get up, and was already wondering what there was to do in the hospital while she waited for news from the doctors. As much as she wanted to stay, she knew it wasn't fair on Becca's family and they would have to come in sometime. After standing hesitantly for a few moments, she hurried back to Becca's side quickly before leaving, just so she could bend down to kiss her on her forehead. That's when suddenly, she noticed her Becca's eyes flickering. She jumped back and held her breath, too alarmed to shout or breathe. This was a miracle! Warm tears spilled down her cheeks as she finally gathered herself and leant forward again.

"Becca?" She whispered. Her eyes slowly opened. She very slowly pulled herself upright, and looked around everywhere before she looked at Jasmine. She observed the pale white ceiling, then lowered her gaze to the heart rate monitor beside her, then even lower still to the green linoleum flooring, then up and saw the comfy-looking blue visitor chairs...until she stopped...on Jasmine's face.

Her first thought was: *What's going on?*

Becca was almost unable to stop staring at this girl's murky green eyes. She thought they were beautiful. On top of that she had the most radiant, naturally tanned skin, and long sleek black hair. The dimples in her cheeks were presented boldly at this moment, because she was smiling brightly. *At me?* Was she Indian? Native-American? She wondered. *Am I?* She looked down at herself and realised, unfortunately, that she wasn't. To her disappointment again, she felt like she wasn't half as attractive as the girl sitting beside her bed. She jumped as the girl finally spoke, feeling embarrassed that she had stared at her for so long. The girl however, didn't look like she was the slightest bit offended.

"Hey, beautiful." The girl said, smiling and showing off two dimples, but slightly choking back tears with her words. "How are you feeling?"

Becca checked herself over. She felt good to be honest, except for a slight ache in her leg and a headache- from what? She couldn't remember. Having already answered the question in her head, she forgot to reply to the girl. Instead she had her own questions, which she asked softly.

"Could you...um...Could you tell me where I am? And, uh...Who you are?"

Jasmine stared at her, mouth open, in awkward silence.

Becca tried again. "W-Where's my mum?"

Jasmine may as well have been stabbed for all the pain she felt when Becca uttered those words. She let out her breath in a sigh of utter disbelief, and managed to choke out a counter-question. "Are you messing around with me, Becs? Your <u>mother</u>? Why on earth would you want her...? This isn't a time to be messing around..."

Becca only stared back with puzzled eyes, and that brought Jasmine's tears back all over again. That was the moment when she suddenly realised, it wasn't really "her" Becca lying there anymore. No way. The replica was clever and realistic-looking, well made; but there was no more love and no more hate, no passion at all inside that empty shell - nothing that made Becca the girl she used to be. She felt like she'd just been cursed. Now, someone she loved so much, had just abandoned her in this world all alone. With a sudden surge of frustration and grief, she smashed a jug of water and all the cups off the side table in frustration.

"How could you? How could you do this to me?"

Becca jumped and her heart rate monitor went wild, grabbing everyone's attention outside, and they rushed in. Jasmine didn't hear it and continued smashing up everything she saw, everything that came in contact with her angry, aching fists. The nurse burst in and tried to restrain her, crying out: "What happened here?"

"I don't know!" Becca cried back, now sobbing with fear. "I don't even know

23

who she is, she just went crazy. I just don't know, I don't know, I don't know..."

She cried into her night gown and covered her ears from all the commotion, so confused, and so scared. When Harry and Gina came in, Jasmine finally stopped dead in her tracks, mid-throw. She dropped the glass fruit basket, SMASH! On the floor, then she turned to face the woman she hated as if measuring her up for the fight. "Get out of here," Becca's mum rasped. "How dare you be in here in the first place, let alone come in and make all this commotion! You're acting like a wild dog, Jasmine! Do you behave like this at home?-"

"-Shut up! Just...shut up, you witch. I hope you're happy now! You have your daughter all to yourself. She doesn't remember me!" Jasmine slapped both her arms against the window pane, and it smacked loudly against her hands to emphasise her point. The sound echoed around the hospital like a ghostly wail from someone who had lost all hope. She looked at her hands in bewilderment as she noticed they had become red raw and bleeding. She became a lot more aware of her body after that as she came out of her raging fit, and she tried to calm her heavy breathing, but she couldn't as exhaustion and grief had swept over her. The loud thudding from her chest was the only noise she could hear and she felt like she was going to be sick. Leaning against the glass and sliding to the floor, her eyes connected with Harry. The nurses and a few doctors then arrived and Jasmine hardly had time to catch her breath before they dragged her up roughly and began carrying her away. All this time, Jasmine had been trying to communicate with her eyes, because it was the only part of her body that wasn't exhausted, and they cried out to him. Figuring this was the last time she'd ever see Becca, they desperately implored: "Please take care of her."

She was too tired and too upset to argue with the hospital as they put her in a new room, sedated her, and she slipped into a long, deep sleep.

Chapter 2

The truth really does hurt.

Every girl has that one person they'll never get over...

The person that was worth waiting for, even if it took all their life, just to fight away their nightmares and wipe away their tears. And in every one of the moments they share with that special person, it seems like nothing else matters as much as being in that one person's arms. Jasmine was one of the loved up fools who felt like this, as you may have gathered, and Becca was "that person."

Their story actually begins a whole two years back, before any notion at all of black motor vehicles or broken bones, as Jasmine was standing at the gates of a new school in this new town. She knew this ritual all too well, and how she dreaded it. Every time she saw the gates of any new school open, it felt like she was just being thrown into a new pack of bloodthirsty wolves. She wondered how anyone ever managed to actually learn anything in high school with all the madness going on within those walls. Here was the place that could easily make an amazing person as well as break one. While everyone else had their little cliques, Jasmine knew she never really fitted sweetly into any of them, and that constantly pushed her into the spotlight as usual, which was one of her downfalls. Everyone was always trying to figure her out. As the school bell rang she hurried inside, clutching her school books intently. The likes of William Shakespeare and Oscar Wilde were her only friends at that moment, and as she entered the noisy classroom she pretended to read the covers of their books rather than meet the eyes of her new rowdy classmates. Fortunately, before anyone could talk to her or ask any questions, the Social Studies teacher flounced in. She was a beautiful woman with blonde hair, big cloudy blue eyes and a warming smile...someone who was always covered in jewellery, feathers or trinkets, and someone the students loved because they could get away with so much with. Jasmine had met her yesterday over the weekend with her dad. She had commented on Jasmine's looks, saying that she had very beautiful, striking features. They had come to the school for a short interview to discuss why she had moved schools, so that meant she and the teacher were the only people who knew- and she intended to keep it that way. This is where she met Becca, the person worth waiting for, and this is where all the trouble began.

"Good morning, darlings!" The teacher chirped, throwing herself down into her desk chair. "How are we today?"

No one replied. Half of the students were still gossiping away to each other, sitting on their desks rather than their chairs, chewing gum and texting on their mobiles.

The teacher, still smiling, began writing the day's topic onto the whiteboard; completely unfazed by their behaviour. *"Modern Romance"* - *Ms Harris*. Eventually when she knew she had to start the lesson sooner or later, she sat down and pouted sadly.

"Come on, guys, you make my job hard enough as it is." She said quietly.

Jasmine never expected anyone to pay attention to her in a million years. But magically, as they caught her eyes, they all settled down immediately, and some even apologised. Ms Harris went straight back to her beaming, happy self, and Jasmine stared on in amazement and awe. It was almost as if Ms Harris felt Jasmine's unfamiliar stare more than anyone else's, because she turned and met her gaze with a wink. Her arm stretched out and she beckoned her forward. "Boys and girls," She continued in her soft, sultry voice. "We have a new student in our lesson today. Her name is Jasmine. Come up here, Jasmine, say hello."

Reluctantly Jasmine made it to the front of the class, keeping her head down even when Ms Harris placed a supportive hand on her shoulder.

"Hello." She muttered. *Why do they always do this? It's SO embarrassing. I wish I hadn't have worn this stupid green dress.*

"You sit right here, darling." Ms Harris said cheerfully, ushering her into her own chair. "I'm sorry we can't play 20 questions to get to know you better right now, because we're a bit behind. But get involved as we move along, won't you? I'd really appreciate that."

Jasmine nodded and as Ms Harris moved away she quietly blew out a relieved sigh to be out of the spotlight. "Today's lesson, as you can see, will be about Modern Romance. I want to know what you teens think about it. I don't know if any of you remember the days when romance could come out of something as small as a guy opening a door for us, and yet no one these days performs these small pleasantries. Is chivalry dead, or just hiding? What do you think, kids?"

A chubby girl with red hair, right down to her ankles, was the first to speak. "Johnny bought me a sandwich the other day..." she said thoughtfully, and a few people snickered.

"...Who here expects a prince one day?"

"It would be stupid to think you could attract a prince," A girl with thick black glasses preached: "If you don't make yourself into a princess."

"Very nice, Vera! Do your parent's opinions play a part in who you go for?"

30

"Probably the opposite. If my mum ever had an opinion of one of my girlfriends I'd run as far away from that one as I could." A cocky looking guy in a sports jacket replied, leaning back on his chair.

"<u>One</u> of your girlfriends, Nathan? Do you have many?" Ms Harris gasped, poking fun at him. A few of the girls in the front row all turned to him at once, throwing deadly stares. He shrunk into his seat, clearly wishing he could disappear completely, and an awkward grin spread across his face.

"I <u>do</u> think chivalry is dead, miss, I think most boys these days are losers." One of the girls in the front row said, clearly to get her own back. The others vehemently agreed.

"Sometimes I can't even be bothered with boys..."

"Ah! Well, that brings us to my next point. Does the behaviour of the male species affect the up-rise of homosexuality? Are we more open to gay and lesbian people now than we were in maybe, 10 or 20 years back?"
Oh no.

"I was only six 10 years ago, miss," Someone joked, making everyone laugh.

"I don't think people choose to be homosexual." Vera said, frowning.

Please don't do this to me, Ms. Harris. I'll do anything. Jasmine tried communicating desperately to her teacher in her head, but it was never going to do any good.

"No, you're right." Ms Harris corrected. "But a lot more people are experimenting more than they used to."

"I wouldn't mind having a gay friend," One blonde girl piped up from the back. "It might be kind of...cool."

Please don't make this day about me, Ms Harris. I really, really don't want anyone to know...

"Well that's very good, my angels," Ms Harris said. "Because I wouldn't want any bullying to come out of you guys knowing that Jasmine here is a lesbian."

Jasmine could feel all eyes on her again, and the class went very quiet. This time, they were not friendly or welcoming like they had been when she first walked up. It was different, just like in her last school. Suddenly no one knew what to do or what to say, like an alien had just been placed in the room with them. She had the horrible feeling in her stomach again that told her that from this day forward she would just be "Jasmine the Lesbian" instead of anything else. She looked at Ms Harris with pitiful, pleading eyes, and knew she had only been trying to help...but Jasmine could not help hating her a little at that moment. *How could she do that to me?*

"...Ew." Said a girl. The very girl that had just said a few minutes before, that she wouldn't mind having a gay friend. A lot of people in the class began to snicker again, then laugh, then full out shouting and jeering began as she became the new freak of the class.

"Do you fancy me?" One girl laughed.

"That's why you left your old school! Did they kick you out?"

"Did you fall in love with everyone?"

"Do we have to be in the same shower rooms as her, miss? I don't want her...touching me..."

The school bell rang but it seemed like the class didn't even hear it, they were too busy thinking of insults to try out on Jasmine, and evil pranks they could begin playing on her every day for the rest of her school life, as she sat there, mortified. Ms Harris tried to settle them, but this time they were out control...hooting and howling like a vicious pack of predators. Jasmine grabbed her books and rushed out of the classroom, breathing heavily from embarrassment and a heavy pain in her heart, leaving the pathetic insults and comments behind her as she fled to the girl's toilets at the end of the hall. Her fingers were still trembling from the ordeal as she locked the door tightly and pressed her back towards it while she caught her breath. She could hear the walls literally humming with all the gossip being spread about her outside, getting louder and louder as a group of girls entered the bathroom.

"I think I saw her come in here," said a squeaky voice.

"Ok, good. Now all of you go wait outside, will you?"

There was more shuffling of feet and Jasmine could hear herself almost wheezing with fear, having flashbacks of the torture people at her old school would put her through, and wondered what horrible trick they had up their sleeves this time. People were always the same, bullies were bullies, and no matter what school she had run to it always hurt just the same. She closed her eyes and silently pleaded over and over, looking up at the dirty beige ceiling. Please go away...please go away...I haven't done anything wrong, please just leave me alone...

"Are you there, Jasmine?" A voice called out, interrupting her thoughts. Her eyes snapped open.

"Y-yes. What is it?"

"I just wanted to see if you're okay. They were really rude in that classroom, weren't they? I just want to talk to you."

Jasmine looked around her toilet cubicle, clutched the walls and tried to steady her breathing. Eventually though she decided the voice seemed friendly enough, and finally she gathered the strength to open the door. The first thing she saw was a girl staring intently at her, with a crooked smile. She was the same height as Jasmine, but she was chubbier, and had short black hair. All her clothes were black, accompanied by dark makeup and a lip piercing. Something about her made Jasmine start to shake inside again, and she gripped the door for support while she tried to figure out what it was. On closer look, she noticed to her dismay that the feature she had regarded as a crooked smile was more like a horrifying grimace.

"So this is the lesbian girl?" She called to her friends outside, then turned back to her. She moved a step closer, and without thinking Jasmine moved left to get away from her, but that just meant she was in the middle of the room now without anything to hold on to. She tried not to think about the girl who was now looking at her up and down and circling her.

"So do you, like, fancy me or anything?"

"Uhm, no. I don't like you...in that way. Thanks."

"Oh? So what, I'm not good enough for you, is that what you're saying? Because I thought you'd be up for it with anyone."

"Well, you thought wrong."

"That's what lesbian girls do, right?" She sniggered.

Something within Jasmine snapped and she suddenly starting blurting things out in a flash of frustration and anger.

"How dare you! It's just like being in any other relationship. You obviously know nothing so why don't you just keep your nose out?"

There was a stunned silence from the girl and she seemed to be staring into Jasmine's core, which chilled her all over. She suddenly wished she hadn't snapped at her, because who knows what she could do in these dirty cubicle toilets with her friends standing guard outside? She closed her mouth like it had just been slapped, which judging on the girl's face, is exactly something she looked as if she wanted to do.

"I-I'm sorry."

"So you should be. Because I <u>know</u> you were looking at me in class."

Jasmine looked at her, suddenly puzzled. This girl's eyes were screaming out to her that they wanted to be reasoned with, or even lied to, which was very peculiar. For a homophobic person, she was acting very homosexual. Jasmine knew for a fact that she'd been concentrating on other things, and hadn't looked once at this strange girl. She figured though, that if she was going to get out of this situation without getting beaten up, she would have to play along.

"I...yes. I was looking at you. All through the lesson." She stammered.

The girl's eyes lit up, and she smiled a genuine smile this time. "I knew it. I KNEW it!"

Something about the way she was talking was more frightening than anything she'd ever heard or experienced before. At least with a normal bully she knew they would kick the school books out of her hands or steal her lunch money - and that was awful enough - but this girl seemed unstable and erratic, and she had no idea where this was going.

"Kiss me, then, if you're a real lesbian. Go on!"

A lump formed in Jasmine's throat and she felt utter terror racking her body. If this was an attack made by a boy on a girl, everyone would be on the scene helping her, so why weren't they now? She glanced up at the girls eyes again and remembered that she would have to play along if she was ever going to escape, so slowly...she leant forward towards the girls' exposed neck. Her lips were inches away from her. She could feel the girl's excited breathing, making her chest rise up and down faster than normal, and the smell of alcohol and cigarettes almost made her heave...but she was doing ex-actly what she had to in order to get out of this situation. Her lips were almost brushing the girls neck, and Jasmine could feel the girl's ea-gerness. But as soon as she felt her guard drop-Jasmine flung all her weight into her- smashing her hand into the Goth girl's chin then rush-ing out as fast as she could, with tears stinging her eyes. The group of girls outside tore after her when the girl finally rallied them, making up some story of course that Jasmine had tried to attack her, but Jasmine couldn't care less. She had to get out of this school, and she had to get out now. This was one of the moments in her life, like many other occasions when bullies were chasing her, that she was thankful she was so small. When she dashed out of the front doors, she skidded to the left and jumped back, hiding behind two large bins. The girl's rushed past, looked confused for two-seconds, then got called back inside by the teachers. When the doors closed, Jasmine sighed out and shut her eyes tight to stop every emotion she had from flooding out: fear, em-barrassment, shame, and relief- then when she had steadied herself she managed to sneak off the school grounds. She ran to a place that had recently become her sanctuary in this busy new town, because it was hidden away from most of the bustling neighbourhood noises and faces. It was the seaside, on a rocky ledge overlooking the placid blue sea and the rock pools where all the small kids played. Jasmine had loved the scenery before, but she couldn't enjoy the view as usual this time. Instead she had her head in her hands and her eyes shut tight, trying not to hyperventilate.

Suddenly she heard soft footsteps behind her and jumped, spinning her head round fast.

A girl she hadn't seen before was right next to her, and she jumped just as much, her eyes opening wide with shock. Her arm was outstretched as if she had wanted to tap her on the shoulder, and she was crouched as if she had never meant to startle her. Jasmine breathed heavily and watched closely, waiting for an insult or some kind of attack, but instead the girl smiled and quietly sat down beside her. She brushed dirt off of her pale blue T-shirt and shorts, then cocked her brown head of hair to the side gently, watching Jasmine as much as Jasmine was watching her. Eventually, she laughed to end the tension.

"I'm Becca." She said.

"...I'm...Jasmine," She replied nervously.

"I was in the car when I saw you up here, so my dad dropped me off. This is my spot, y'know." When Jasmine seemed apologetic, Becca laughed.

"I just came to see if you were okay, really. Saw you crying."

"Oh," Jasmine blushed. "Yeah. I, er... didn't have a great first day at school. Eastbridge Secondary, do you know it?"

"Yeah, I go there. Just had the morning off because I went to the dentists. I'm really sorry you had a bad time."

"Not your fault."

"What happened?"

Jasmine paused, searching the girl's eyes for any evil. Should she tell her about the girls? In her head a tiny voice said no, that was too much information to put onto someone else's shoulders, especially since they had just met. There were certain people who Jasmine had encountered through life whose personalities

41

would turn the moment they found out about her, too, using any information like that against her, so she figured it probably wasn't the best idea. As she searched this girl's eyes though, she found nothing but curiosity and kindness, which really shocked her. Her heart leapt a little as she remembered her prayer from this morning, and wondered if Becca would be the person to understand everything.

"The...The class found out that I'm not into boys. At all." She said eventually, and looked at Becca worriedly through her long hair, hoping she could read between the lines. She did. "Oh..."

Jasmine actually stopped breathing then, because she knew all her hopes of finding a new friend relied on what happened next. Is she going to freak out and run away now? She wondered, already pitifully losing hope. But then Becca said something that changed Jasmine's whole world.

"Is that it?"

This little town was not exactly the most modern place in the world. Many people were still stuck in their old ways, never adjusting to any change- so Becca understood why maybe her classmates had acted so badly towards her. But she liked to think of herself as better than all of that. Perhaps it was because her mother was the head vicar in church that she had always rebelled to what was considered "normal" in life, but things like that had never, and would never bother her in the way that it did to others.

"It's not even any of their business. You shouldn't ever be ashamed of who you are, or worry that you're not like everyone else. Too many people spend time on pretences, and that's the thing that's really weird in this world."

Jasmine had no words to describe her happiness. She couldn't even look Becca in the face for fear that she'd explode on her with some strange form of pent up-emotions. Tears? Laughter? She didn't know. Becca watched her face and smiled slightly, glad that she could help out someone with her words in this way. She slapped a hand on Jasmine's knee however after a while, hating to have such a heavy conversation with someone she'd just met. She hated all sad things in general.

"Tell you what. I'll come in with you to-morrow, hmm? That would show them. They wouldn't <u>dare</u> tease you if they knew you were with me. I've kind of built up a reputation over the years...I'm not to be messed with. So don't worry about a thing."

"...'Cos every little thing..." Jasmine muttered, grinning.

"...Is gonna be all right!" Becca laughed.

Bob Marley.

It was plainly inscribed in the stars that from then on they were going to be amazing friends. The image of Becca at that moment, with her sparkly blue mischievous eyes and windswept brown hair in its messy ponytail would forever be implanted into Jasmine's mind. That one image of her in Jasmine's mind, even 2 years on, was the one where she always remembered when Becca looked like the most beautiful girl in the world.

Chapter 3
Justice is…nice.

The next day at school, Jasmine stood again at the gates of that same new school but this time it was different. The kids made their jokes as they passed her by while she stood there in the cold, clutching her school books just like yesterday, but this time the difference was that she couldn't hear them. She was too contentedly blind and deaf to their remarks because of the fact that someone was coming, to walk by her side and be her friend. Before she could even blink that thought away, she felt warm hands gently pushing her forward into school, and a soft voice said beside her, "What are you doing out here? It's cold, y'know."

"Becca!"

"Hey. Sorry I'm late, but that's kind of my thing. I didn't miss first lesson, did I?"

Jasmine didn't even realise she'd been standing there that long. "Oh, not if we rush." The first lesson was Geography, but the teacher wasn't in and with a substitute in place instead, it was practically a free lesson. Although the ditzy teacher was a pro in Maths, he spent half the lesson trying to figure out which way up the map went. Becca spent most of the time watching Jasmine, who was watching other people laugh and whisper about her.

"Hey, Becca!" A boy named Carlos called out eventually. "Do you know that girl is a lesbian?"

Becca paused, then faked an exaggerated gasp and clutched her chest, pretending to have a heart attack. "Thanks for alerting me." Jasmine giggled, then stopped abruptly and began to blush when more people started to stare. Becca put a hand on her shoulder.

"What would your mum say?"

"You run and tell her if you want." Becca laughed, sticking her two middle fingers up at him. She then turned to Jasmine, and explained before Jasmine could ask. "My mum's the vicar in this town, and a strict one at that.

If she knew I was hanging around with a lesbian? Damn, she'd have my head."

Jasmine blushed a deep red. She didn't want to ask this question, but her curiosity got the better of her. "Why are you, then?"

She shrugged. "You looked like you could use a friend. I'm not going to let my mum dictate who I can and can't be friends with. Or Carlos, at that. Even though I am a little scared of my mum finding out, there's no way I'm going to let him know that!"

Something warm filled up inside Jasmine. "Thank you."

"No problem."

"Guess you'll be wanting your new mate to join us on the squad, then?" Another boy, John, asked.

"What? Oh, no I don't think so." Becca eyed Jasmine up and down in a football-analysis kind of way and figured that by the delicate little dresses she always wore, she wasn't much of a footy girl. "I might be off for a couple of days, y'know...just to show Jas here around and make sure you losers are treating her nice from now on. All right? She's with me."

There was a united moan from the whole of the class. Hell, it seemed like even the substitute teacher, who had given up and was now eavesdropping, was shocked when he heard this, too.

"But-but...we need you!" John said quickly, starting a cheer. "Come on, Becca!"

"Sorry, guys. You'll just have to manage without me, just for a little while. There's not even any big games coming up."

"Your little girlfriend will be just fine! We promise! If you just come back onto the team-"

"What did you just say?"

"You're already calling her 'Jas', that's a bit pally don't you think? You should be careful, you don't want her getting ideas..."

"Yeah! Look at the way Jasmine is looking at her, already! It's sick!" Carlos piped up again.

Becca jumped up and grabbed him, then slammed him against the wall repeatedly until he squealed. It was so quick that the substitute teacher hardly had enough time to jump up and say, "Ey..!"

"Watch what you say." Becca said, quietly but menacingly.

She was usually the coolest person in the class. The joker of the football team, and the friendly female face, with skills to match. But everyone knew not to get on the wrong side of her, because football wasn't the only place where she could match a guy's strength.

"Y-yeah, Carlos." John said shakily. "Becca can have all the time off she wants."

There was a chorus of sound from the class-mates that gave some indication that they agreed, and she let him go just as the school bell rang for break time.

Becca cheered a little and was out of her seat before most people, eager to get out into the open air for the usual 15 minutes, but Jasmine seemed stuck to her seat and staring hard at something, or someone, and so Becca's mood dropped slightly.

"You all right?" She said, genuinely con-cerned.

"Uhm, yeah...of course," Jasmine smiled awkwardly. "I just have to do something quickly. Can I come and meet you outside in a bit?"

"Okay, sure."

Becca bounced off to the playground. Jasmine continued staring at the girl who'd tried to assault her yesterday. She was staring right back, but something in her eyes was desperate, and almost afraid now. They sat quietly until the teacher packed up his things and walked away, and then the girl came and sat next to Jasmine. Jasmine quickly dropped her gaze, wondering what she wanted, and feeling awfully uncomfortable.

"Hey, I see you came back," The girl said nervously.

"Yes, well people like you don't scare me." Jasmine lied in reply.

"I wasn't meant to scare you or anything, y'know? I mean, if you ask my friends they'll say 'Oh, that's just Anna being her crazy self.' I just got a bit carried away, I think. And I'm really sorry."

"I don't think that was just getting carried away. Do your friends know you're a lesbian too?"

Anna cringed at the word and jumped back as if someone had set fire to her leg. "I-I'm not! Don't say something like that to me!"

Jasmine rolled her eyes and sighed. "Okay, fine. Thanks very much for the apology, if that's what you want to call it...it's accepted. I guess I'll see you next lesson."

She collected her things together and started to get up, but the girl jumped up too and grabbed her arm, telling her to wait. Jasmine stared at her hand touching her in shock and disgust again, until Anna let go and they both sat down again.

"Jasmine...you're not going to, y'know... tell anyone about this are you?" She said, as if the words caused her pain.

"No. I'm not a grass if that's what you mean. I would never tell the teachers. And most of the kids here still hate me, so..." She trailed off as a thought hit her. As she looked at the girl now, as opposed to yesterday- at the way she was being so slimy and embarrassed, on the borderline of scared- she realised something. It seemed like she was more scared of a certain person finding out more than anyone else. Jasmine had caught a glimpse today of the respect everyone in the class had for her newest friend, because she was confident and fierce, but she hadn't realised just how much

51

of an impact she had on her fellow classmates until now.

"You're scared of Becca."

"No! Well...yes. If she found out the whole school would be against me! Not to mention she could knock 10 pounds out of me if we ever got into a fight."

"Why is that my problem? Maybe you <u>should</u> find out how it feels to be me for a day."

"Please. Please, don't. I'm begging here! Look, I promise me and my friends won't ever bother you again. We'll go back to being the Goths in the corner, you won't even notice us. If I knew you were friends with Becca I would have never...I mean...please, please don't."

Jasmine was smiling inside just watching her squirm like this, and her respect for Becca was growing every second. A part of her wanted to ruin this girl for what she almost did to her, but a bigger part of her didn't. She figured that that would make her just as bad in any case, but she was glad that the girl had somewhat realised her wrongs.

"I won't. Okay? It's over, so just leave me alone now."

"Thank you, Jasmine. You're actually quite cool," Anna grinned, flying out of her chair before Jasmine could change her mind. "I'm sorry again...thanks so much."

She grabbed her bag and ran out into the corridor to meet her friends, while Jasmine stayed glued to her seat, still in shock, but basking in the glory of what had just happened.

Chapter 4
She'll be the one to comfort you

Jasmine remembered that she could hardly sleep the first morning Becca said, in her most sweet and innocent voice, "We can walk to school together tomorrow, if you want." She'd been awake long before the sun had even risen, pacing up and down her room, checking herself out in the mirror and sprawling her potential outfits all over the room.

Chill out, a voice in her head said.

Too late, her heart replied.

She knew it was too soon, and she was definitely rushing into things, but she felt like already she was starting to have feelings for Becca. It was hard to differentiate whether those feelings were just friendly or romantic yet, because it had been a long while since she'd had a lover, or even just a friend. All she knew at this stage was that Becca was the only one in the town that was worth anything to her, and because of that, she deserved all her attention. She didn't even stop for her dad's famous breakfast omelette, which hurt his puppy pride a little, but she promised that she'd make it up to him later. If she could have flown to Becca's front door she would have, but instead she had to make do with skipping, and her smile couldn't have been any wider if it tried when she rung that doorbell for the first time. When Becca's front door creaked open, the greeting she got wasn't the one she expected, to say the least.

"Shhh!"

Becca looked out on the street while peeking around the corner of her door before ushering Jasmine quickly inside. She hurriedly helped Jasmine take off her coat then tried to gently push her into the living room, but Jasmine caught herself against the door frame and spun around suspiciously. "What's going on?"

"I can't really tell you." Becca said sadly. Before she could protest or say anything else, Becca disappeared into her kitchen. Jasmine was about to follow her when another voice startled her and she spun around yet again, looking into the living room at a figure on the sofa.

"I'd just give them a bit of time if I were you, babe."

Jasmine was so startled that it made her sit down involuntarily in the nearest seat. "Oh, ok. Sorry."

A tall boy was sat in the sofa, playing a fighting game on his xbox and was still in his dark blue pajamas. He had shaggy brown hair that almost covered his eyes, but their friendly brown colour underneath was too handsome to go unnoticed; and he had a light five o' clock shadow around his mouth. He hadn't looked up from his game as he talked, but he seemed friendly and easy-going, so Jasmine re-laxed as she realised he wasn't telling her off as much as advising her.

"I'm Harry," he said quietly after. "You might have seen me around school yesterday. Becca's twin."

"Oh, really?" Jasmine piped up, intrigued. "I didn't know she had a twin."

He laughed. "Well, that's Becca...only interested in herself."

"I'm Jasmine."

Harry's game ended and he was finally able to look up at her. He smiled the most debonair smile Jasmine had ever seen. "Well, it's nice to meet you, Jasmine. Cor blimey! You're a tiny thing aren't you?"

"I don't think so..." Jasmine frowned, "...maybe you're just tall."

Harry laughed. "I'm really sorry you've come today, because I'm not sure Becca will be able to come to school with you. We have...family issues...and it's her turn to sort them out."

Jasmine's heart sank. "Well, can't I help out too?"

"It's difficult. Just take a listen at the door and I'm sure you'll change your mind."

Jasmine ran to the kitchen door as soon as she had permission. She was determined that whatever I was couldn't be that bad, and she would do anything to get that walk with Becca to school. The one she'd imagined so many times in her head. She pressed her ear as close to the door as she could without troubling it.

"Where the hell has your father got to?"

"Mum, please. Stop this. You know dad's not coming back, why are you doing this to yourself?"

"He will be here. I've made him breakfast, see?"

"Where are your pills, mum."

"I don't need them! For Heaven's sake, if you don't get your father right now I swear I will..."

"He's gone, mum! He's got someone else now, please...just don't do this..."

"Get out. Go and find him. Go and do your homework. Go and clean your room, and we're going to church later. Just go! Now! Get out!"

Becca suddenly burst out through the kitchen door and almost crashed right into Jasmine. She ignored their collision and turned sharply, with a key in her hand to lock the door on her mum. Then she fled into the living room and

Jasmine could do nothing but watch and follow behind.

"I've locked her in, there's no reasoning with her on this one," She said sharply to Harry as she walked in. "I don't know what else to do, I mean I can't find her pills. We're going to have to call them for her."

Harry nodded solemnly, and picked up the phone. It was only then, behind muffled talk of psychiatric assistance, that Becca focused again on Jasmine. When she turned to her, Jasmine saw that her face was red and her eyes were teary, even though she tried her best to hide it. "Sorry, Jas. There's a lot of stuff going on at the moment, y'know? I'm sorry. Did Harry tell you that I might not be able to come with you today?"

"Yes, but in that case, I'm staying here with you."

Becca blinked in surprise. "Really?"

"Definitely."

"God, that's so kind of you. Are you sure? We could get in a whole lot of trouble."

"Oh, it's okay. I'd much rather help you out then go to school alone."

"Thank you so much." Becca smiled warmly, then gently clasped her hand to show her the way up to her room, where they could hang out for the day. Harry just got off the phone and watched them walking up the stairs together.

"Later, Pipsqueak," He yelled, and Jasmine cringed as she took off her shoes at the bottom of the stairs.

"I hope he doesn't stick with that nickname for me."

Jasmine considered Becca's home a palace compared to the run-down apartment where her and her father Archie had just moved into, still riddled with moving in boxes all around the place. She was particularly astounded by her bedroom, however. It was more pink than she had imagined, but the essential parts were characteristically Becca's. She had a low bed in the corner with an unkempt white duvet hanging off the edge of it, facing a desk and a window. A tiny brown teddy bear who looked like he'd seen almost as much as Becca had in his life, sat lightly on the top like the guardian of her pillow. When Becca caught her looking at him, she smiled goofily and tucked him away out of sight. The desk was scattered with unfinished homework and doodles, underneath a small stereo and a laptop. There were a few shelves above the bed which held a few unorganised school books and pictures in frames, and an awe-inspiring, overworked guitar that stood grandly in the corner. But the most prominent feature was the range of posters stuck up against her walls, almost covering every inch.

"I really like your room," Jasmine said cheerfully.

"Thanks. Just looks like an old dump to me."

"Who are these people on your walls?" Becca smiled and went over to one in particular. "...All my favourite female footballers. Especially this woman here. Siobhan Chamberlain, wow. I think she's amazing, and I hope I can be as good as her one day for sure."

"Cool."

"Who is? Me or her?" Becca laughed.

Jasmine laughed. *You.*

61

"What about you? What do you want to be when you're older?"

"Oh," Jasmine blushed. "A Nurse."

"Well...!" Becca guided Jasmine to the bed so they could sit down to talk. "Now that's a noble profession. Let's hope we stay friends so you can patch me up whenever I get hurt on the pitch, hmm?"

"Sure," Jasmine laughed in reply.

"Did you like my brother?"

"Uhm...Well, yeah...he's okay. Very friendly." Jasmine was a bit confused by the question, or rather, the tone in which Becca had asked it.   "When you say 'like' you mean...?"

"Oh, of course! I'm sorry. I totally forgot you were into girls instead. I'm just used to my friends coming here and falling head over heels for that silly guy."

Jasmine smiled, then let her hair fall over her face to hide the blushing.

"W-What's it like? Y'know. To be interested in girls?"

"Just the same as liking boys really. Except...if you fall for the wrong girl, it gets hard. For instance, a girl who's straight? It leads to all sorts of troublesome things. The worst thing boys will do is tell you if they don't fancy you. But girls will tell you, then tell their friends, and laugh about it, then spread horrible rumours for a few months afterwards."

"Sounds awful. So why do you like them?"

"Not them, really, I don't fancy just anyone. When I first realised that I was attracted to a girl, it was just the one girl who changed everything. It was all about <u>her</u>. I knew from the moment I saw her that I had feelings for her, and admired things about her like her confidence, and her beauty. Unfortunately, she was one of the girls who were awful to me, broke my heart, and drove me here."

"I'm so sorry to hear that."

"It's okay. I've met you, and you're even more wonderful."

"Oh, really?" Becca burst out laughing, in a nervous way. "I'm not anything special."

"You always look so confident, and everyone in the school seems to respect you."

"I don't think they would if they could see the real me. The one sitting here, with you, with the crazy mother downstairs. Maybe I've

63

become a bit stronger because of that, always having to look after my mum when she goes into her little episodes, because I can feel Harry always looking to me. That's the burden that comes with being 2 minutes older, I guess."

"I think you're doing fine."

"...Thanks."

Jasmine watched Becca's face for a while, hoping she would explain what was going on a bit further. She knew it was just what she needed right now: a friendly face, and a friendly ear that was willing to listen. Thankfully Becca didn't need any more prodding than that, and exploded into a speech about the whole issue.

"My mum has had this... problem... for quite a while now. I'm not exactly sure what it is, but all I know is that since my dad went away, it's been getting worse. Sometimes she gets delusional, sometimes she gets angry at me and Harry for no reason at all...and it's almost impossible to stop her when she goes off on one. She's violent too. I've been trying to get her to take her pills but she doesn't listen to me. I actually hate it here, I hate how she tries to control everything we do when she's normal, and then still puts a huge burden on our lives when she's not. The only reason I stay is because Harry won't come with me to live with my dad, he loves my mum too much and I'm still baffled about that one, because all she's been is awful to him. I just wish...that it was someone else. Why did I have to have this life?"

Becca sighed and stared up at her ceiling for a second, obviously trying hard to push back some hard emotions. When she lowered her head however, it was as if nothing had happened, nothing had been said, and she was back to her normal bubbly self. "Look at me, harping on, when from what I've heard of your life, mine is nothing in comparison." She smiled and pulled Jasmine a bit closer onto the bed, then pulled the duvet over the both of them. Jasmine jumped inside when she felt Becca's touch, but held it together and breathed slowly to calm herself. Her left arm tingled as she felt it leaning against Becca's, and she couldn't believe she was with someone she liked so closely, and in such a short space of time. Becca was also feeling a weird sense of closeness between the two of them, but she accepted it happily as the feeling you get while sharing thoughts with a new friend.

"You do know this means you're my best friend now, right? I wouldn't have told all this stuff to just anyone, it's just that for some reason I feel like I can really trust you. That makes you best friend worthy."

"Oh, ok..." Jasmine blushed. "Best friends."

Becca looked as if she was about to lean in for a hug but Jasmine looked away, politely but quickly, before it could happen. She would never be able to hold her composure then. She cringed slightly, hoping Becca wouldn't notice that her body was screaming wildly for her, like a magnet to a fridge. She'd promised herself that she was never going to make the same mistake as she did before, because Becca was straight and she didn't want to get hurt again, so she planned to keep her distance.

"...Have you had a boyfriend before?" She asked quickly, in a squeaky voice.

"Well, not really. This guy at school has really liked me for as long as I can remember, his name is Nathan. We've never done anything together. In fact, subconsciously I think I just keep him hanging on to annoy my mum. He's a great guy and everything, a really close friend, but I just don't feel that way for him."

"I see."

There was an awkward silence in the room suddenly that Jasmine could not understand, but she watched Becca closely and could almost see the cogs turning inside that brain of hers. Her eyes flickered up and met her gaze, but just as quickly they looked away again. *She's embarrassed*, Jasmine figured.

"So umm...with all those people talking about us at school yesterday, it seems like we're the new biggest attraction. But umm...was that all ignorance? Or do you really fancy me?"

With a sigh, Jasmine struggled to calm herself before all her blood rushed to her face. "I do."

"Whoa."

"But listen! Before you freak out- I'm so sorry, I didn't want it to come out like that. I know you don't feel the same for me and that's absolutely fine. I mean, I'll try my best, and I can wait...and wish...but it's absolutely fine, I promise. I don't want to lose you as a friend now, I can't."

"Hey," Becca put a supportive hand on Jasmine's shoulder and smiled. "It's totally fine. Let's not be so dramatic."

Chapter 5
You think you know a guy...

"Ahem."

Jasmine's eyes snapped awake, and she quickly drew the hospital bed covers up over herself. Oh no! *Take me back to those days*, she thought anxiously. *I want to live in that moment forever.* Unfortunately, she was back into the reality of the present moment, and she wondered if it was because the drugs had worn off. In that case, she really wanted more ASAP, so she could go back to sleep and back into the world of flashbacks and memories. Here, she remembered that she was in a hospital room, two doors away from her girlfriend that didn't even remember her. Everything about the situation hurt. She hated what had happened, and she hated hospitals. The fact that her door was always opening here was one of the worst things about it all as well- there was forever someone sticking their nose into her room, whether it be a doctor, a nurse, her father, or just some weirdo who'd wandered in by mistake. She felt like her eyes were deceiving her at this moment however, because a boy with handsome brown eyes and shaggy brown hair entered the room, the one boy with those features who she had expected the least.

"Harry?"

"Hello, Pipsqueak," Harry said, as a nurse rushed in to prepare a seat for him. "I came to visit Becca, but I heard you still weren't out of here yet either so I thought I'd pop in."

"Thank you so much! That's so nice of you. H-How is she today?" Jasmine said quietly.

"She's doing just fine, thanks. Seems to be healing really well."

"I knew she would be. Don't tell anyone but I've snuck in there a few times when she's sleeping or when she's knocked up on meds, just to see for myself. I miss her face. She's so beautiful."

"Jas! That's the worst idea I've ever heard. What if she wakes up? She'd totally freak out!"

"Yeah, I suppose so. But it's only me, it's not a murderer."

"Hmm......The nurses are saying that you might stay in here longer than she will. That's bloody ironic."

"Yeah, I know. Weird, huh? They've got me on every drug they could find in here. They've diagnosed it as Broken Heart Syndrome y'know, it feels awful and is hard to cure, but they're working on it."

Harry laughed. "No, really. What's happening?"

"Well, honestly...It's because they're worried that if I go home this soon I won't eat. I hardly eat anything here as it is because I can't while I feel like this. And so because i'm... well...petite, the doctors are worrying. I told them all not to though! It's so silly, but that's generally why I'll be here for a while."

"That sounds terrible. I'm really sorry. You really do have to eat though, Jas, otherwise you'll disappear!"

"Thanks for the concern." She giggled.

"...That breakdown you had a few days ago was so unlike you."

Jasmine paused. "It's not everyday that the person you love gets run over, then forgets you exist. I mean, what are the chances? What on earth did I do to deserve that?"

"It's not your fault, hon."

"Maybe it was. I mean, I gave her the coat, and she would have been able to see better if it the damn hood hadn't been over her eyes...she would have heard the car, and would been able to run..."

"No. Don't even start thinking like that. Some things just have to happen. It's not fair and you probably won't like it, but that's life. You just have to work with what you have now."

"...Okay. I'll try." Jasmine thought about it for a while, then smiled. "I bet her memory will come back in a few weeks anyway, and I shouldn't worry myself."

"Well..." Harry fidgeted uncomfortably. "That's not really what I meant..."

Jasmine looked at him, first with hope, but then her smile faded as she looked into his eyes. "Is it...is it really bad? What have the doctors said? It <u>will</u> come back, right?"

Harry drew his chair closer and gave her a hug, but said nothing. Jasmine tried to take that as a "we'll see." rather than the worst things that were whirling around in her head.

"All the stuff we did together...everything." She whispered. "Our first Valentine's Day, all those moments up at the beach..." She choked back her words when she realised that saying any more things like that would just start her off crying again, so instead she paused, then tried to focus on the good things. "At least when we both get out of here, I can tell her. Or better yet, while we're in here together. Yeah! As soon as she wakes up later on, I'll go and tell her everything. She won't be scared anymore, and hopefully it will trigger off some-"

"No, Jas. You can't."

"...What?"

"I'm so sorry, but you really can't do that. I mean, she's doing so well, we don't want anything to upset her right now. I just want her to get better and get home."

"Well of course! I mean, I want that too. But...I wouldn't upset her. You know I wouldn't. She's my Becca, she'll be happy the sooner we're back together."

"I don't think there will be any getting back together, Jas. I love you like a sister but it's just that...well, things are better if she doesn't remember. Not that I don't like you, you understand? And I wish you too could get back together. But Mum hasn't had one of her episodes in a whole week, and she's so excited about when Becca comes out and we can start up afresh, y'know, as a family. You understand that that's a bit more important than your relationship, don't you? We can finally be a <u>normal</u> family again."

"Are you serious?"

"I'm really sorry, Jasmine."

"Is that why you came here then? To tell me all this? Because wow, silly me, for a moment I thought you just came to check how I was. How can you be saying this, I don't understand it, Harry, why are you doing this to me?"

"I have to think about myself here."

"What about yourself? Is this because you don't have a girlfriend right now, that you can't understand? That's pathetic. I thought you of all people could see how much I cared for your sister. I need her, more than you'll ever know. She's all I have."

Jasmine stared at this stranger in the room with her. He was someone that she thought she could always trust, but now he'd turned, just like everyone else in her life, and she couldn't bear it. She felt herself starting to suffocate under the immense pressure that was building inside her head, and her skull felt like it was burning from the amount of tears she was trying to hide from him. She was determined to keep whatever dignity she had left, and there was no way on earth that she was going to let him see her cry.

"Get out." She whispered, not looking at him.

He didn't move an inch until a single tear slid down Jasmine's warm cheek. After a short pause, he reached up slowly and tried to wipe it away with the bend of his index finger.

"Get OUT!" She yelled, exploding with anger and hurt once again, slapping away his hand. She scrambled to the corner of her bed before he could try to touch her again, because his fingers felt like knives to her vulnerable, betrayed flesh. And she screamed. She pulled the emergency cord on the hospital bed and she screamed until he ran out in shame, and screamed until the doctors came in and he was out of sight. Then, having used up all of her lung capacity, she flopped on to the bed and shut her eyes tight, trying to drown out the alarm sound and the thousands of questions from the doctors that seemed to never end.

Chapter 6
Partying their morals away.

Some of the school days went by in a blur of paper and aimless chitchat for Becca because she had daydreamed so much in lesson, only emerging from her coma to see if Jasmine was okay, once in a while. Thankfully most of the time she was.

It was three weeks to the day since she had arrived, and while Becca kept a protective wing over her, it seemed that she was adjusting well and even starting to enjoy herself. Becca was happy that her influence had helped her in that way, and when she thought about that in History class she found herself smiling. It wasn't until Jasmine glanced sideways and noticed the smile that Becca's cheeks filled up with utter mortification, thinking about how goofy she must have looked, and she couldn't look again for a good long while after that.

After school, the girls were just putting on their coats and idly chatting with others in the common room before they went home, when a small scrawny brown-haired boy came rushing in, whizzing in and out of the crowds like a little mouse. He jumped onto a table nearby, and everyone turned around almost instantly. This was because, the boy wasn't any ordinary nobody. He was Kevin, the "assistant" of one of the coolest boys in school- Nathan. Coolest, or hottest, as most girls felt he was. He was captain of the football team, and a beautiful dark coffee colour, with hazel eyes and striking muscles. And whenever Nathan sent his assistant, it meant that something amazing was about to happen.

"Boys and girls!" He yelled, but everyone was already silent. "Don't forget the theme is "Damsel in Distress" for tonight's party!"
Everyone began whispering excitedly as Kevin jumped off the table and disappeared. Becca seemed to be the only one who was shaking her head in utter bewilderment, and slapped her hand against her head.

"Oh my god, I totally forgot!"

Jasmine popped her straw into a carton of juice and took a slurp, while observing her with innocent wide-eyes. "It sounds exciting."

"Yeah, I don't know what on earth happened to make me forget. I have to get my outfit together! You coming?"

"Uhm," Jasmine twiddled her long hair between her fingers. "I didn't get an invite. I don't even know the guy."

"Oh come on! Me and Nathan are very close. Remember I told you about him? I can introduce you. He won't mind, and you'll love it, I promise."

Jasmine's heart jumped as Becca grabbed her hands as she tried to persuade her, and that was definitely enough. They left school together shortly after, and went to Jasmine's house when Becca had picked up an outfit from hers. They had a tiny picnic on Jasmine's bed, waited on by none other than Jasmine's dad, Archie, who was a big kind hearted guy who made them laugh all the way through. He was so happy to see Jasmine make a new friend.

In the evening, the moon had already began to rise up through a purple sky when they left for the party. It created beautiful streaks of pale light that wound it's way in and out of all the back lanes in the neighbourhood, like silk. The two girls ended up in front of a massive front door with green stained glass windows and loud music playing inside. Becca rang the bell, then turned to Jasmine, quickly examining her. She looked like a Greek goddess, with a long flowing white T-shirt dress and a golden band around her head. Jasmine caught her gaze and they both smiled at each other.

"You look amazing," Becca said softly, just as the door opened suddenly. She cringed as she noticed who had opened the door at that particularly embarrassing time. A tall young man had opened the door, and the lights and music poured out of the house. As soon as he saw them he began standing defensively against it, seizing up in utter mortification. Becca was equally embarrassed, thinking that he had heard was she had just said to Jasmine, and was preparing himself to tease her about it in about five hundred different ways. But weirdly, it wasn't because of her. Nathan had his own guilty conscience bothering him.

In the next few uncomfortable minutes, a girl with long black hair in a high ponytail, brown eyes and a beer in her hand appeared. She was laughing at something that had happened inside, and began falling against him until she too saw the girls, and her smile faded.

"Hello, Becca."

"Hey, Gemma. Nathan. You two look...cosy..."

"...So do you two!" Gemma protested guiltily.

There was a weird little silence where the two pairs just stood silently, staring each other down. Eventually Becca sighed and turned to Jasmine, who looked astounded at the amount of tension there was already, and they hadn't even walked through the front door yet. "Well, this is awkward. You see, Jasmine...standin' in front of you here is my best friend, and my prom date, falling over each other like a sordid Romeo and Juliet. And they have the cheek to be accusing me of something, instead of letting us in so we can forget about this and enjoy ourselves. I'd much rather do that then stand here and have this conversation, wouldn't you?"

"Yes." Jasmine nodded vehemently. She hadn't known Becca for a long time, but she could tell from the heat radiating out of Becca's ear like a steam train, that if they all didn't drop this soon she would explode...and it wouldn't be pretty.

"I-I suppose we'd have had to tell you sometime..." Gemma muttered.

"Tell me what?"

She knew it was a stupid question, because the answer was written all over their faces. The situation quickly calculated itself inside Becca's brain, no matter how much she tried to push it out. Because it couldn't be possible, could it? She closed her eyes tight and fought off waves of nausea. *My best friend. My prom date. No, no way.* She couldn't focus on anything at all except the made up scenario she'd dreamed up of them together - kissing, touching...it was so wrong that Becca wondered if there was a helpline she could call. This happened to other people. Not her. The next wave of emotion flooded her senses. Anger. This was not a situation she wanted to happen today.

"So you are two together now?" She snorted. "I spend a week showing a new person around the school and you two do this to me? Wow. I really never expected that." She turned to Nathan, who was looking very guilty and hadn't said anything. "But you don't fancy her. I know you don't fancy Gemma, Nathan. You told me. You said that even though you knew she fancied you, I had nothing to worry about, remember? What happened to us, and Prom?"

"I really did want to go with you, Becca, but I'm not blind. I can see that you and that girl aren't just 'getting to know each other'..."

"But Gemma's my best friend! Couldn't you have found someone else? What did she have to do, open her legs for you?"

"Becca!" Gemma gasped angrily, crunching her beer can in her hand.

"No! Whore! How could you, how <u>could</u> you?"

Almost in slow motion, Jasmine suddenly felt herself in the middle of a fierce fight. She saw Becca leap forward off her toes, arms outstretched, as if her only deadly intention was to rip off every emotion from Gemma's face. Gemma was being held back by Nathan, but insults were flying out of her mouth faster than a computer could process them, and she flung the used beer can brushed past Jasmine's face in an attempt to hit Becca. The insults were both about Becca and herself, which gave her terrifying flashbacks of other times at other schools where people had attacked her for her sexuality. Becca suddenly pummelled into Jasmine by accident, taking all the wind out of her. Somehow she managed to hold her ground, and dragged Becca away by her shoulders until her and Gemma couldn't reach each other anymore. She was still punching and kicking with all her might, blinded by rage. Jasmine kept pushing Becca back, restraining her, until they were almost out of sight of the house. Becca was almost in tears now, and continued to call out horrible things to the couple, but they couldn't hear it. Jasmine guided them to her seaside hideout above the beach, making sure she was always in front of Becca so she couldn't run back and start trouble all over again, until finally they both ran out of energy and collapsed together on the sand. Minutes passed, and the only sound between the both of them was heavy breathing and light sobs from Becca, along with the rolling in and out of the peaceful tide. Jasmine's chest heaved up and down while she looked up at the stars, trying to think of something comforting to say, but she had nothing. Becca finally managed to calm herself now that she was out of the situation, and now more than anything, she felt embarrassed that Jasmine had had to see her in that state. She sat up slowly and checked Jasmine over where she lay on the sand. Jasmine felt her stares, but was too afraid to move or look back. It hurt Becca the most to see Jasmine act that way to her, so in some form of consolation, she touched Jasmine's face and brushed her hair out of her eyes for her.

"D-did I hurt you?"

"No."

"I'm so sorry, Jasmine."

Jasmine sat up beside her, and saw her face full of shame. "You don't have to apologise. I'm okay, really. I just hope you are too." She nodded. "It was just a little bit of a shock. It's amazing how quickly everything can change. Especially because of just...one person."

Jasmine blushed furiously, to Becca's mortification. "No! I didn't mean...I'm so happy I met you Jasmine. I'm happy everything's changed. Really."

After a pause, Jasmine hid a tiny smile under the hair that had fallen all around her face. It gave her the best feeling in the world to know that Becca appreciated her. She flopped back onto the sand, exhaling a big breath of air, and Becca followed her, smiling too.

"I had this fantasy anyway," Jasmine shrugged. "I hoped that maybe, if no one else had asked you, that you'd come to Prom with me."

"...Oh."

Becca was speechless for one of the first times ever. She hid it well though, styling it out by putting her hands behind her head, and pretending that the question hadn't made her stomach fly up like she was on a roller-coaster ride.

"I'm sorry. I know that was a bit forward." She whispered.

"No, no. It's fine."

Jasmine didn't mind the avoidance of the question, because silence was much better than a rejection...especially with what she planned to do next. There was something in the air tonight that was so special, she hadn't regretted asking it for a second. A part of her was so glad that this had happened, because they had never had such a raw moment alone like this before, with the emotional tension so high and out in the open. She had never felt so close to anyone in this way before in her life, and she loved it. The beautiful night had entranced her and as the sun set, the warm glows from the park lamps seemed candlelit. She engulfed herself in Becca's musty scent. They seemed to be protected from the heavy drumming of the outside world here in their special place, caught between some temperamental sea waves in front, and calm rustling trees far behind. She closed her eyes and gathered strength from the place, feeling the sand and grass run melt underneath her fingers as she shifted her weight, then sat up and began to lean over Becca. One of her hands slid over her waist. Her hair fell against Becca's face and she felt as if she had captured her and brought her to the same place in her heart that she was at that moment, where nothing else mattered. Becca froze.

"I-is this too forward?" Jasmine gulped quietly.

"No. It feels weird, but...fine with me." Jasmine tried for a laugh, but her heart jumped at the same exact moment so her laugh came out as more of a gasp.

"Don't stop now," Becca said shakily, peering into her eyes, with a childish sense of wonder. Becca was surprised but intrigued at the same time, and a force within her didn't want to move away at all. She found herself mesmerised by Jasmine's lips, and how they pouted sometimes in a sexy way without warning, talking to her in a silent, sensual way. Without breaking eye contact, Becca dropped her hands down and put one on Jasmine's neck, and tenderly stroked the back of it. Jasmine smiled and slipped her own hand into Becca's other free one, then leant forward so their lips were so close that you could hardly slip a paperclip between them.

"I meant to thank you, for saying that I looked amazing today. It meant the world." Jasmine whispered, brushing her lips against the side of Becca's face as they talked.

"You do."

Suddenly then with a sigh, Becca sat up. She had interrupted the moment and was now back angry again more than anything else, because on that note she was reminded of what had just happened with her best friend and Prom date. "I can't believe some of the things Gemma just said to me. Selfish? A bitch? If speaking my mind means I'm a bitch...if standing up for myself is selfish...and if admiring a girl makes me a lesbian...then yeah, guess I'm all of those."

Jasmine laughed.

Becca grinned back. "So, Ms. Grant...are you worth me leaving my old life behind for?"

Chapter 7

Oh, what a nice new life!

Becca opened her eyes slowly, disturbed by the faint sound of muttering in her room, and found herself in the presence of five people sat around the bed. They all turned to her with the same glassy stares and plastic smiles, as if this was a scene from some mad freak show involving porcelain clowns.

"Hey, Becs." A boy said, smiling at her. Becca stared up at him and remembered her brother, Harry, but only because of the whole incident when she first woke up. He had such kind eyes, and the way he looked down at her was with nothing but love, and worry...but on the other hand, Gina sat next to him and her face was almost the opposite. She looked like she was uneasy about being here. She tried to ignore it and smiled back at Harry. "Hey."

"Did you sleep we-"

"Shut up, Harry, let the doctor speak first." Her mother snapped suddenly. Harry looked as if he'd been smacked hard across his mouth, but held his head down and didn't say anything. She sharply nodded at Becca as if to say hello, then turned to the doctor. "She can come home today, right, Dr. Lewis?"

A doctor with long black hair and lovely brown skin coughed nervously. "Uh, yes. All your vitals are recovering very well, so you should definitely be able to go home today."

Gina beamed, her eyes glassy and cold.

"That's great," Becca said. She then turned slowly to the face on her right. She was a beautiful girl, with pale skin and black hair. It took a while but eventually thoughts and memories flew back into her brain and she was able to recognise who she was.

"Gemma?"

She shrieked. "You remember me! Oh, thank God. We've done too much stuff together, I wouldn't even know where to begin telling you if you'd forgotten me."

"No, I haven't. I remember a lot of things about us, but not everything. I don't understand why I feel this kind of hurt in the pit of my stomach when I look at you. It's weird."

Gemma shifted anxiously and glanced at Nathan next to her, who was looking at his feet.

"It...it can't be 'hurt'. I mean, that's a very strong word! Me and you are best friends forever, right?"

Becca paused, then smiled nervously.

"And you're Nathan. Hey, I remember a lot of people telling me that you liked me."

Gemma frowned. "You must be mistaken, Becs. I go out with Nathan, remember?"

Becca wished people would stop asking her if she remembered. The doctor's beeper suddenly alarmed and she graciously made an exit, along with Nathan and Harry who figured that whatever was going to happen next didn't really involve them. Becca peered anxiously at the door, wishing Harry would come back because for some reason, she didn't feel very safe with her own mother and best friend alone in this room.

"Now, darling. There's obviously a few things we need to talk about before we take you home." Gina leaned forward, clasping her hands together. "We never answered all those questions you had, about the...the..."

"Jasmine." Gemma added helpfully.

"Yes. Let me tell you something about that girl. I promise you, baby, she's been nothing but trouble since the moment you met her."

"Oh?" Becca blinked. "So I knew her?"

"Yes, but she was no one to you. Nothing. Unfortunately, though, she seemed to think she was, and that's the worrying thing. What I'm saying to you, Rebecca, is that she was *obsessed with you.* You used to tell me all the time how you wanted to leave this place just because of her, and how you hated being followed around her. Isn't that right, Gemma?" She nodded vehemently.

"Gemma was your real friend. You must remember how good she was to you, and how she'd never do anything to hurt you, not like that girl."

"I just want to see you better, Becca," Gemma interjected softly, taking her hand. "I miss my best friend and just want to see her back to her old self."

93

"I-I am. I'm trying to get better, really. You don't have to worry." She tried to reassure the both of them. "If you think this girl is bad news for me, then I won't see her. It's no problem."

"Yes, yes, good. One more thing, too." Becca looked into her mother's steely eyes.

"She's dangerous. I'm warning you, Becca. Stay away. She's been dangerous before, just look at what she did here in the hospital. God knows what happened to get you in here in the first place, we'll never know will we? Since you can't remember how can we be so sure that she didn't have anything to do with it?"

Becca snorted. "No way."

"This is serious, Becca! Don't mock things like that."

"Okay! Okay." She huffed. She tugged at the band on her arm so hard that for a moment she sheepishly worried that she might break it, and that would only lead to more fussing from the nurses. Something about this whole conversation didn't feel right. The urgency in both of their eyes, willing her to do as she was told was unnerving. She suddenly laughed, something she always did when she felt pressured. "What's the big deal, guys? I won't go near her, okay? No need to go on about it."

Gina and Gemma looked as if they'd been holding their breaths. After a few more painful minutes, Gemma finally responded. "We're just looking out for you."

"I know. Sorry."

"Okay, darling. Gemma will escort you around wherever you need to go, do you understand?" Something about the way her mother said it made Becca realise it wasn't up for discussion. "You will go to work, then come straight back, until things get sorted out, at least."

"What about my house? Can she come to my house?" Gemma added hopefully.

"Ok, fine. But that will be the only place you go."

"Great!" She squealed.

Becca looked at her as if she was an alien, and just couldn't imagine how they had ended up friends. They were so different. Becca could feel that in her gut already, but didn't say anything as she watched her mother exit the room, and pretended to be interested in Gemma's ramblings about hair and makeup. Something big was missing here, she just couldn't put her finger on it. There was a white space around her that seemed to be distorting her image of everything, like a picture that had been ripped right through the middle. She knew they couldn't keep an eye on her every hour of the day, so sooner or later she would go out and find someone who would tell her the truth. Hopefully that would be the person who could fill the void as well.

Chapter 8
Damn it, she didn't want the truth.

Jasmine had been comforted only with her few precious memories for a while in the ward of the hospital, until a frequent and familiar visitor popped his head around the door, with a huge smile and a bunch of pink flowers.

"Dad," She sighed.

Archie did his comedic walk into the room as he always did, as if to say: "Is it safe?" and "I'm going to make you smile today." That was typical of him. When he had swept over and cleared the distance between, he kissed her on her forehead, placed the flowers in his lap and took a seat.

"How is my angel today?"

"She's ok. I suppose."

"Better than yesterday though, huh? I hope those nurses got you to eat something after all that fuss."

Jasmine stared into space, hoping he wouldn't press anymore on the subject.

"The restaurant is doing well at home, you know. It's a madhouse in there these days! I went with what you said, I put that new curry on the menu and everyone has been flocking in for miles."

"Well there you go, I always knew you were a genius, dad." She turned to him, and tried for a smile.

"No! Without you I wouldn't even have thought of it! You are the genius. Oh, and also...my team won the match on TV this past Wednesday. That one I'd been waiting for about a month...?"

Jasmine made a disgusted face and stuck her tongue out, making him chuckle.

"It really wasn't the same without you in the house, screaming: 'Keep the noise down!' from upstairs." He said, laughing harder.

A tiny giggle burst out from deep down somewhere within Jasmine, where a part of her still had a sense of humour, and it made her shake her head with disbelief.

"You can always make me laugh, dad. Thank you. And I know you're trying to make me feel like I'm missed, which I really appreciate, but I can't really do the small talk thing with you right now. Becca left the hospital four days ago, and I was trying not to ask you about her, but you know she's the only thing I want to know about in this stupid town."

Archie sighed. "Okay, pumpkin. I understand. But you know anything I have to say will make you upset, right? So why ask? Why not just get your strength back and come and chase her yourself?"

"It's ok. Just tell me."

He fidgeted. "Well...Gina has her convinced that she was a regular little church girl. I usually now see her in pretty little dresses, skipping down the road like there's nothing in the world that can bother her. She's even getting along with her now...very well in fact. Gemma is protecting her as fiercely as a German Shepherd would, making sure all the right people say all the right things to her. Nothing about you, I mean. Nothing that reminds her of the past."

Jasmine's whole body had stiffened where she lay in the hospital bed as her father talked. The images that flashed into her head due to his description was something out of a freaky Stepford wives conspiracy.

"Why isn't anyone doing anything to stop it?" She whispered.

"I'm sorry, pet. It seems like no one cares except, well...me, and you."

"I see."

There was a terrible, awkward silence in the room after that, and Archie could just see the frustration and hurt rising up again inside Jasmine. Her head was held low and she seemed to be burning a hole into her bed sheets with her eyes. Archie brushed a hand through his streaky black and grey hair, desperate for something to say, but he came up with nothing. Instead, he grabbed her up into his huge arms and made sure without words that she knew he was right there with her. In case she'd forgotten.

"You're just going to have to fight this, love. If Becca is really everything you want."

She wiped her tears away on his sleeve before he could see, and talked even though his arms almost muffled the words. "I've been fighting to be who I am all my life. What's the point of being who I am, if I can't have the girl who was worth all the fighting for?"

Archie chuckled, a sly chuckle from deep in his heart. "Whoa. At that moment you sounded just like your mother. Up until the very day that she died, she'd been fighting for certain things that she believed in most."

"What things?"

"Oh, loads of things! Mainly political, but you are missing the point. You already have all you need inside you whenever you become ready to get your girlfriend back. Do you understand me, young lady?"

"Like what?"

"Well...A heart of gold from that mother of yours. With it you can be brave, and strong, and the gold will shine bright enough to stun all the people who question you."

Jasmine laughed. Sometimes Archie was so dramatic.

"And...! You have a traditional Indian fire-belly from me. Not only does that mean that you can eat hot foods, my dear, <u>oh</u> no...it means that as soon as you start to believe in yourself, insults will never bother you, just as peppers don't."

"Awww."

Archie loosened his grip on her and she relaxed back onto her hospital bed, finally feeling a little better.

"That should be your aim if you insist on being here. Focus on the good things that could come out of this! You two will both be so much stronger after this, you know that, don't you?"

Jasmine nodded, but wasn't really so sure.

"Of course! I hope you remember this advice in about seven years time, when the both of you are adopting. I'd quite like a grandson named Archie, Jr."

Jasmine giggled. "Sorry, Dad...I was thinking more along the lines of Joel if we have a boy. As for girls, Maybe Jade and Jacklyn? I want to stick with a "J" theme. That's four already, and I think that should do it, but you never know. I want to move away from here too. Somewhere much sunnier, so I can have a swimming pool and a nice garden. Maybe with just flowers, or maybe learn a thing or two from you and plant herbs and peppers! I'd make sure we came and visited you every month, for sure. I'm hoping I can pay for you to get a much bigger, better house as well. We could all even go for super family holidays! How about Paris? Disneyland? I suppose we'd have to get a huge car too then, wouldn't we? I hope my children are talented because I'd love to be a perfect mum and take them to all their piano lessons, and baseball games...Oh, listen to me! You're getting me all excited now. I haven't felt like this for the longest time, thanks so much, Dad. It's great to look forward to something now for a change. It's so lovely to dream about these things, isn't it? I shouldn't get so carried away though. I mean, we've still got a long way to go before we're at that stage. When the time comes we'd have to talk about it a lot more. I'll definitely have to make sure everything I've said is okay with Bec-"

Jasmine suddenly plummeted back into reality. "...Becca."

Archie put a comforting hand onto her shoulder, and that was the point when she couldn't hold it together anymore. Her sobs came out in awful bursts, almost choking her, and Archie had to hold her again because he was afraid that she'd hurt herself by the way she was shaking. At first Jasmine could hear him talking to her, trying to make everything better in that special way he usually did, but at that point she was already too lost in grief, and the voice soon faded away. Though she couldn't comprehend the time in her state, she stayed there for what seemed like hours, just crying into her father's arms.

Chapter 9
There's something she needs to know

Back in the days when Becca remembered who she was and who she was going out with, she rode home on her bike after school, grabbed a bite to eat from the kitchen then burst into Harry's room. He was listening to music in his headphones and almost fell of the bed with shock when he saw the door open so quickly.

"Hey! -" He exclaimed.

"Look, there's no time for you to tell me off, I've gotta talk to you." She said, ignoring his protests and finishing off a muffin stuck between her teeth.

When he had caught his breath, he glared at his sister before rolling his eyes. "Go on then."

"I have feelings for someone. A female someone. And I'm wondering what to do about that."

Becca's matter-of-fact tone gave him the impression that if he laughed or made the slightest snide comment, he would be in for a beating. But also, knowing how hard it was for her to open up about her true feelings to anyone, he reckoned these feelings must be serious.

"That girl you brought around here the other day?"

"Who else?"

"Does she swing that way?"

"You know she does."

"Then I say go for it."

With that, Harry began to lay back on his bed, and closed his eyes while plugging his headphones back into his head. That's when he felt a hard *thwack* from a pillow on his stomach.

"She likes to read," Becca said quickly, suddenly breathing heavily. After a puzzled pause, Harry sat up and scrutinised his sister carefully.

"You're nervous." He gasped.

"I am not. Do you think I should buy her a book? Y'know, to read?"

"You're nervous!" Harry said again, jumping up. "Wow, this really must be serious.

I can't believe it! My own sister! The great Re-becca Jameson is-"

"All right!" Becca snapped. "Of course I'm nervous. I haven't exactly done this before. And I...I really, really like her, Harry. God, she's so adorable sometimes. I know I've had boyfriend's before but nothing even compares to the way I feel when I'm with her. She's the smartest girl I've ever met, I think. You should see her in class, she has her hand up for every question...especially English. She knows the whole of Romeo and Juliet off by heart. And she makes me laugh so much. We like the same foods, we're always together..."

"And...?" Harry said quietly when she trailed off.

Becca sighed. "She's just...so beautiful to me. Every time I've been near her recently all I want to do is cuddle her, kiss her, and just pro-tect her. All the time! I don't want to imagine my life without her, I want to give her the whole world...and I would if I could..."

Harry scooted over to his sister and put an arm over her shoulder. "Okay, sis. Honestly, you're just working yourself up for nothing.

I'm sure she feels exactly the same, and you don't have to worry."

"I know she does, she's just been waiting for me to catch up I suppose. But here I am now, ready, with no idea what to do. Or say."

"Just use that natural charm of yours, Beansie. It's worked with everything else so far."

"What have I told you about calling me that?"

"Sorry- habit! Now piss off already, I'm trying to listen to my music."

Becca laughed and made for the door. Just before she closed it completely, she peeked back in to see her brother had sprawled himself back into position on the bed, hands behind his head, relaxing the day away.

"Thank you Harry," She whispered.

He made a small "hmm" noise without opening his eyes, knowing that it was hard for Becca to say that to anyone, so he didn't want to rub it in or make it into a soppy moment. But when she finally closed the door properly, a smile swept across his face.

Chapter 10
She's mine.

The next day at school, the bell had just gone and it was now the beginning of lunch. Becca had sat through Maths class with her head in her hand, part-daydreaming, part-sulking the whole time because oddly Jasmine had not been in today. Just the day when I need her the most, Becca huffed. But eventually, as she picked herself up and walked out of the classroom, her heart leapt 20 metres when she saw Jasmine finally, holding a few books as usual, bounding happily towards her.

"Hey!" She said happily. "This school is great! I've was trying out for the decathlon team. I just need to let Mr Burgis know and show him this note, then I'll come meet you, ok? Where we usually sit?"

"Huh? Oh, okay. Sure," Becca smiled.

"Are you okay? You're very quiet today."

"Really? Just thinking about stuff, I guess."

"Okay then. Well, I'll see you later." Jasmine smiled, showing her dimples and making Becca tremble inside. Then when Jasmine touched her arm then went bouncing away down the corridor, the tremble turned into a sharp pain, brought on by worry.

Did I just miss my chance? Oh, God, maybe I wasn't supportive enough just then. Maybe she thinks I don't care now, maybe she doesn't like me anymore and might find some new friends and maybe she won't even come back to meet me here for lunch...

"Jasmine!" Becca yelped, in a higher pitch voice than she'd expected.

Jasmine spun round at the other end of the corridor, with one hand on the door. She looked confused but like an angel to Becca nonetheless. Her shiny black locks fell around her face, her green eyes sparkled with curiosity and her flowing beige dress spun and wrapped around her. At that moment Becca decided that nothing could be more right than what she was about to do.

"I love you!" She yelled.

The impact of the sound waves of those three words knocked Jasmine backwards a bit. Other people in the corridor fell into stunned silence but Becca couldn't have cared less. She was staring into Jasmine's eyes despite how far away they were from each other, trying to tell her with eye contact that she wasn't messing around, and hoping she felt the same. Jasmine stood awkwardly as if she didn't know what to do with herself, but her chest began heaving suddenly and before she knew it, she was struggling to contain her sobs.

"I love you." Becca repeated, quieter this time, but with the same conviction. She felt her feet move, and before she knew it she was walking forward towards Jasmine. Jasmine echoed the moments, and soon the both of them were almost running to each other, until they crashed in the middle and Becca had her in her arms. The people around didn't know whether to look away in disgust or stop and stare, but that was what the majority of them were doing. Becca swept her hand across Jasmine's face gently, feeling the dimples from her smile as she nestled into her, and her eyes wandered up and down her small elegant frame in a suddenly exciting and new way. They were so close that both of them could feel the heat from each other's breathing as they looked at each other, having a loving, silent conversation using only their eyes. Jasmine began to say something but as her lips slowly parted Becca felt the most overpowering urge to move forward and plant her own lips onto them...so she did. Suddenly in the middle of the corridor they were sharing their first kiss: something that was beautiful and weird and dangerous all at the same time. Dangerous because, in a school like theirs, the population could only take so much scandal, even if it was from a respected figure like Becca. The noise from the background eventually became too loud to blissfully ignore for Jasmine, and as she turned around she noticed the frowns and the whispers. She shrunk back from Becca, who then noticed it too. It was a good thing they stopped when they did, because Mr. Burgis then turned around the corner, obviously overhearing all the commotion, and stood at the end of the corridor staring hard at them. Technically they weren't breaking any school rules, but the look from their Maths' teacher told them that he was just waiting for an excuse to get them expelled.

"D'you wanna get out of here?" Becca whispered through her teeth.

"Yes please." Jasmine sighed and she silently thanked Becca for being so in tune with her emotions. She hated being the centre of attention, especially bad attention. Somehow this felt different to all the other times she'd been picked on, however...different to all the times when bullies had kicked her books out of her hands. This time she had someone to share the pain with for the first time. And it felt amazing. Her eyes flickered as something sparked in her brain; something that she had forgotten to say.

"By the way Becs?"
"Yeah?"
"I love you too."

They snuck out of the school, slipping between the hedges in the corner of the baseball field. For Jasmine, bunking off school like this was one of the most exciting things she'd ever done, but for Becca it was a weekly occurrence.

The new type of excitement for Becca was coming from hearing the new crazy thoughts, shouting to her in her head quicker than she could think them in order. Her heart was beating a mile a minute, and something about the way she was looking at Jasmine now scared and excited her. She's mine, Becca gasped, but silently inside her mind. She's really mine!

They finally arrived at Jasmine's house and as soon as they got through the door, Becca cornered Jasmine against it. They kissed again, and Becca had never experienced anything so amazing in her whole life. She felt Jasmine's soft skin under her fingers and explored every part of her like she was a shiny new toy, and in return Jasmine gazed up at her with innocent eyes and let out a tiny sigh.

"God, I want you." She said in the most serious tone, making Jasmine giggle. She mocked a gasp, only half pretending to be shocked, and trying her best to settle her uneasy breathing. If danger had a distinctive smell, she felt that it would be Becca's- in the sweet place between the neck and the top of her chest.

"Don't act like you're the innocent one, Jas. I'm the one that's new at this. And you're the one that looks so...so..."

She couldn't find the words straight away. Maybe it was because she was so distracted by Jasmine slowly tugging on the rim of her jeans and leaning her chest towards her, or because she felt the urge to pin Jasmine's hands above her head, and she was always prone to give in to urges. Eventually she finished her sentence. "...beautiful."

Jasmine could only blush as words failed her completely. Her whole body had shivered in excitement when she had sneaked a look at Becca's underwear, and the bright red, French ruche garment she was wearing was nothing short of her personality. Her lover's blue eyes under her dark makeup seemed to have caught her hostage, and she was could do nothing but watch in excitement when Becca leaned in for another kiss. The kisses were hard and soft at the same time, sometimes followed by short breathy giggles, as if they were both trying to conceal their excitement and not get carried away too quickly. She was more calm about the whole situation than Becca was, and she was good at comforting her and letting her know what felt good and what didn't. Watching Becca taking the lead was amusing, because it was like she was determined to be in charge even though she'd never been in this situation before. Jasmine made the softest glimpse towards her top, and as if magnetised, Becca's hands jumped at the chance to touch there. She put her own hands over Becca's as if to reassure her of what was feeling amazing when she looked unsure. A seductive smile crossed her lips and she steered the pace a little faster. She held Becca tighter still, and even closer, and focused on the good feelings she was getting.

Becca felt like subconsciously she had waited for a moment like this for a very long time, and until now no one had come up to standard. It frustrated her inside that she hadn't done this from the moment they'd met. She'd never done anything like this before, but when she looked up at Jasmine's face, she realised that it was the right call. Jasmine's eyes had captured her completely, and it almost felt as if those big greens had complete control of her. They slowly began to move with each other, rubbing all the right places up and down in their position, as if they were in some breathless slow-dance. Her eyes felt like they'd never be able to break away from Jasmine's face because her features expressed nothing but pure pleasure, and Becca never wanted that to end. Her clothes had never felt so uncomfortable on her before, and Jasmine's dress felt tender on her skin. Sometimes the moves came second nature to her, like when instinctively her hands slid down to Jasmine's waist and caught her just as she gasped and almost fell into Becca's hold- but other times she completely froze and Jasmine had to soothe her with reassuring words, that brought her back into reality. She took a lot of time watching Jasmine as if she'd never seen her before. Just seeing someone enjoying her company so much was enjoyment enough, but certain things Jasmine did made Becca tingle, like when she took sweet deep breaths that blew against the hairs on her neck, and her lips came dangerously close to her own. Whenever Jasmine's lips brushed hers in the most teasing way possible, Becca was sure she stopped breathing altogether.

Just before she slipped into a state of total bliss, the moment was brought to an end with a gentle knocking from within the living room. Her breath caught in her throat as she realised that could only mean one thing.

"My dad's here!" Jasmine hissed, utter mortification in her eyes.

"I hear smooching, but I need the bathroom. Can I come out?" Archie joked.

With that Becca couldn't contain her giggles. They went to greet him, then rushed upstairs to save themselves from further embarrassment.

* * * *

"I know what you want to do now," Becca said in a mischievous tone, winking.

"...Sleep."

Jasmine laughed. "No way."

"I can blatantly see you do. I do too," Becca smiled. "Nothing like a nap after a pig out."

"I wouldn't dare. How could I even think of sleeping when you're lying here with me in my bed? I'm even scared to blink! This is too unreal. What on earth would you see in someone like me?"

"Someone I want to be around always. Someone I would proudly hold hands with in the street, and go to Prom with. I can see myself doing a whole lot of other stuff with you, too, but I don't want to scare you away just yet. Don't you worry, I'm not going anywhere. That's one good thing about my outburst, right? No more secrets or rumours...it was my public promise to you. It'll be just me, protecting you forever, like the most important thing I have."

"Most important? You have no idea how long I've been waiting for someone like you, Becca Jameson. You're not just the most important thing I have, you're the only thing I have. So don't you leave me."

Becca laughed. "I won't! God, you're jinxing us before we even begin. We've got so much to do together, just you wait. I'll always be here to hold you from now on, and I'm going to make you strong. So you sleep now, okay? I have to go home before my mum freaks out, but I'll be with you tomorrow. And the next day. And the next day. And the next day..."

She kissed her new girlfriend and silently slinked out of the room and repeated those last words over and over as Jasmine drifted off to sleep. Who'd have thought, the promise she made on that day would last two blissful years...until that cruel twist of fate broke that promise for her.

Chapter 11
One of many times love beat her down

Jasmine stared at the hospital ceiling as a nurse pumped relaxant drugs into her veins, and while she waited for them to take effect, she thought about one of the very first encounters she'd had with Becca's mother. She wondered what the hell Gina must be saying to her, trying to make her forget everything she was. She looked down at her bandaged hands and wondered if Becca was still thinking about her, even if the only memory of her was at the hospital. Tears stung in her eyes but she tried to hide them as the nurse made her exit, and she waited some more for the drugs to take away the aching pain in her heart, longing for Becca.

She remembered staring up into her father's face from her bed as he tried to coax her out of her bedroom, when he knew she was thinking of skipping work one morning.

"Come on, you get your posterior out of that bed, and show them what the Grant family is made of." He said, grinning.

Jasmine sighed, lifted herself off the bed, and managed to break a smile for her silly father. She worked at the small Diner in town and loved it, but just felt heavy and tired that particular morning as if she knew something bad was going to happen. When she finally made it to the diner with a lift from her dad though, she forgot about her feeling. She enjoyed all the blissful moments when she was serving people their lunch...and watching children's faces light up when she scooped them an extra sneaky scoop of ice cream. About half way through her shift a dark presence entered the room, and before Jasmine could even turn around to see who it was, she felt it. People stopped talking about ordinary things, and laughter subsided. It was Becca's mother, Harry, and a posse of old men from the church. Jasmine gasped so sharply that it sent a pain through her stomach, then turned around quickly before they could see her. She didn't even smile at Harry as she usually did, because she really didn't want to attract attention. Jasmine and Gina had become acquainted more through gossip more than anything else, and from the talks Jasmine gathered that she did not like her. That was enough to give her stomach butterflies, being as self-conscious as she was, let alone the death stares she felt piercing through the back of her apron. Thinking quickly, she rushed over to the counter where her boss was cleaning it.

"Julia, you see that group over there? Is it okay if I don't serve them? I mean, I know you're short-staffed as it is, and everyone's busy...but I just..." Jasmine couldn't think of a way of describing it without bursting into tears and explaining the whole story. Luckily her boss turned to her with sympathy in her eyes, and simply nodded as if she understood exactly why.

"It's okay. I'll serve the vicar and her group myself."

Jasmine was ready to sigh in relief when a sharp voice called out her name, along with a snide remark. She closed her eyes tight and tried to wish them away, but the nightmare had already started.

"Looks like this Jasmine girl has already began preying on another girl than my daughter, instead of doing her job! Waitress?"

Jasmine turned around, grinding her teeth slightly, and walked over to greet Gina face to face. She had sat in a corner sofa seat with all of her friends, and to her they looked more menacing than a group of juvenile teenagers.

"So this is the heathen that is trying to corrupt your daughter?" A brown bearded man said, eyeing her up like she was a piece of meat. "What is the world coming to these days?"

"What can I do for you, Gina?" Jasmine said without a smile, ignoring the man. She refused to get into a religious debate with a person she'd just met about her personal life, in full view of the public even though she wasn't a heathen and she would have loved to shut him up. She could feel Gina's eyes were boring into her flesh, making the heat under her cheeks flare up, and the hairs on her neck tingle.

"There's a lot of things you could do for me. How about not misleading my daughter and dragging her down with you on the path to Hell?"

"Mum, drop it please. Is that really necessary?" Harry asked uncomfortably.

Jasmine's fists clenched up. Even though she was never one to physically harm anyone, and hadn't in her whole life, she would have relished in hurting this woman somehow. It was only the look on Julia's face, filling with pure worry and concern that stopped her from doing something she would have regretted. She released her fists and continued with her dignity.

"Becca is free to make her own choices." She said quietly.

"Not while I'm around. I won't watch my daughter be mislead by bad people."

"Well, when me and Becca were talking in bed last week, she gave me the impression that there's only one person she thinks is bad for her, and it isn't me."

"Talking where?!" One of Gina's friends squeaked. Gina stood up abruptly, fuming, and knocked a few things of the table with her movement. She stared Jasmine down as if the urge to fight was mutual. It was a horrible thing to say but she enjoyed making Gina squirm, even though she knew it was completely innocent- it just hadn't sounded that way.

"Feel free, reverend." Jasmine said as her voice shook. "Let's settle everything in front of all of these people. I can't wait to see Becca tomorrow with a black eye from her own church-leading mother."

"Mum!" Harry squeaked.

"You...stay away from my daughter." Gina said, talking so quietly and closely that Jasmine could smell what she had for breakfast on her breath. "How long do you think you will last in a town where no one wants you? I hope eventually, we drive you out and you end up alone, in a pit where you belong."

Jasmine could not take any more abuse, so in the most dignified way she ignored the comments and simply walked away. A smile slowly formed across her face when no one was looking. Gina had unintentionally just made her day with what she said, and more with more enthusiasm than ever, she was going to work as hard as she could. No one would be able to ruin this day now, and Gina's petty comments were probably just what she needed.

A town where no one wants me? She thought. Wrong. The one person that matters, she wants me. How long do I think I will last? As long is it takes. As long as it takes for me to make as much money as I need to get me and my sweetheart out of here forever. This is the pit, and you don't have to drive us out.

We're already aiming for bigger things.

Chapter 12
Everything she says, hurts.

Jasmine thought that having nightmares was the worst thing to come out of sleeping. But as she opened her eyes and found none other than Gina Jameson sitting by her bedside in the hospital that morning, she realised there was worse things out there than figments of her imagination. This was real. There was no waking up from Gina's penetrative gaze which was steaming right through her, no escaping from the sight of her excessive caked on makeup and red lipstick grimace, and there was no amount of pinching that would save her from the dirty feeling Gina supplied to her. Jasmine's tenseness must have given away all her emotions however, because Gina chuck-led. With a blatant disregard for hospital health and safety, she lit up a cigarette and made it painfully suspenseful in the room before she finally revealed what the hell she was doing there.

"You've got the right idea, Jasmine." She then said. "You should be in an institution of some sort, but just not this one."

Jasmine couldn't breathe, the whole air in the room seemed to have been sucked out by Gina's cigarette and bitter personality. Her fingers twitched underneath the button that would call the nurses in to protect her, should anything happen, but something about the visit was deathly intriguing. Why on earth would Gina come to her? She couldn't help but wonder if it was only to gloat, but even still, at least she would get news about Becca. That was a small luxury.

"How's the service in here? Good? Have people been visiting you? I bet everyone has been pussyfooting around the issue of Becca, haven't they? Well, I had a few moments to spare and I just thought I'd come in to set you straight. She's the perfect daughter now. She does her homework on time, she comes to church with me, and she has real friends again. No time for stupid romances. It feels amazing. For once, she does exactly what I tell her to do.

With no arguments or complaints. It was always her father encouraging her to argue with me, anyway. So now he's not here, there's nothing that can break the new bond we have. He was always the one putting stupid ideas in her head, making her so free-spirited and rebellious. Everything is new now, just the way I always wanted. She will finally do the things I had planned for her."

Jasmine would have given everything to have been able to speak at that moment, and she glared at Gina who was still dragging puffs from her cigarette. Unfortunately though, the nurses had hooked her up with a tube that was pushing nutrients into her stomach because she'd had another episode this morning and refused to eat. There was a lot of sedatives involved. She would have loved to tell her that she was sick, in her head, and that she should really try listening to herself from time to time. It hurt her to think that beautiful people like her own mother had their life taken away while so-called mothers like Gina got to live, continuing to spread their poison on to everything and everyone they touched. Of course all mothers had expectations and hopes for their children, but the way Gina was declaring it wasn't right at all. She would have loved to tell her all of that, but by the way her legs were shaking ever so slightly under her covers, they told her that she probably wouldn't dare even if she did have her voice.

"Stupid Shaun. Thought he knew everything about raising kids. Actually, he thought he knew everything about everything! But he was wrong. Maybe he should have spent less time on them and a little bit more on our relationship, because things could have so easily been worked out. Was I really that unreasonable? He betrayed me, that bastard. I understand you'll be leaving in a week, and I want you to know that there will be no contact between you too. And I mean, no contact."

Becca's mother pulled out a piece of paper from her purse, unrolled it, then pushed it under Jasmine's nose. Her vision was still blurry, but she could just about make out her name and a few other details about herself. She looked at Gina, and tried to express confusion with her eyes.

"A restriction order." Gina said bluntly in reply, rolling her eyes. She then continued in the most patronising voice Jasmine had ever heard- it was almost a song that you would use to explain to a three-year-old.

"It means you wont be seeing my daughter anymore! Is that clear? Because it says you can't, right here."

Jasmine made a small noise under her mask, and Gina's plastic smile slowly began to drop as soon as she realised it had been a laugh. She pulled back, away from Jasmine's face, and slowly but deliberately folded the restriction order up and put it back into her bag. Her face should have been a picture just then, but the more Jasmine watched her the more scared she was becoming. "The legalities were just so the whole neighbourhood would know about you, and be watching when I'm not around. We both know the real reason you'll stay away though."

She tapped her cigarette onto Jasmine's pillow, then stubbed it out on her dressing table, and Jasmine recoiled in disgust. "My Harry came to see you, didn't he?"

She asked, relaxing a little into her chair. "That was brave of him. I have been real hard on that boy, ever since he was little. I just automatically suspected that it would always have to be him I would have to look out for, the one of both of them who would be the most...sinful. May have had to do with the fact that Shaun adored him too, I couldn't bear it, especially when his affection for me was decreasing so rapidly around that time as well. One day when Shaun was not home, he had taken Becca out...and I stayed in with Harry. We were sitting at the table and I asked him: 'Do you want to say Grace?' He looked at me, and I'll never forget the moment...he looked at me and asked 'why'. Why? Why would he ask that? And how dare he! He was so young that I knew it wasn't his own idea to ask me that, but all the same, it was a mistake I had to make sure he'd never forget. I saw red. There was just something in me, some deep hatred perhaps for his father more than anything else, that saw his rebellious nature rubbing off on my only son. So, you know what? I burned him. I had to teach him a lesson. I took his tiny arm and put it over the burning stove... and told him never to question me again."

Jasmine stared into space, in shock. The room felt empty and quiet for a long while, and even Gina sat stone-like as Jasmine processed all the new information. Eventually the feeling came back to her hands and they started trembling, then she began sobbing, and the tears of regret came streaming fast down her face. It almost made sense to her now, how Harry always acted so brainwashed to his mother's wills, and she was so annoyed with herself for not considering some form of abuse earlier. Suddenly Gina leaned forward, making Jasmine jump. She had a new plastic smile on her face again as if what had happened, didn't just happen. Jasmine's eyes darted around the room, pleading with God that there was a security camera in the room. As she spotted it she could only hope that it was on and functional at the very least in case Gina decided to do anything to her, because praying that there was sound on the old thing was too much to hope for. This time when Gina talked, her voice was very low, and extremely sinister.

"If I could do that to my own son, you should be worried about what I might do to you."

Chapter 13
Some things subside, but never disappear

"It's almost time for church, Becca, are you ready?" Gina yelled from downstairs.

"Yeah mum! What's up with this stupid dress?" Becca yelled back.

Gina held her breath downstairs, pausing from even stirring her tea. For a moment that sounded just like her old daughter, the one who NEVER wore dresses and was NEVER ready for school on time. The daughter she'd lost a whole three months ago. She feared the day that maybe, as the doctors said, she might get her memory back. But after listening out, and realising that Becca was still fumbling upstairs and putting the dress on, she breathed a sigh of relief. She liked this new daughter so much more. It was so nice to have a clean slate, and Gina loved making up stories and getting Becca to live them out like the daughter she'd always wanted. Not the sinful, free-thinking creature she had spawned and hated before the accident.

Upstairs, Harry walked into Becca's room forgetting to knock, and witnessed Becca with a frilly pink dress seemingly stuck to her head. "Hey, let me help you." He rushed in, laughing.

"You're supposed to knock!" Becca screamed, pretending to be angry but laughing too.

"Sorry, Beansie, you know I always forget."

After pulling her dress down for her, he sat on her bed and gestured for her to come and sit down next to him. Before she did, she took a bit of time to study her twin brother. She still hadn't quite gotten used to his face again yet, but whenever he spoke, his voice gave her a warm sense of home and family. She knew that Harry was someone she could trust, and unlike your usual quarreling brother and sister, they seemed to get along very well. He had very honest brown eyes and shaggy, mousy brown hair on top of his head, just like hers. He was much taller, and reminded her of a lamppost with eyes all the time, which made her laugh. He came across way more friendlier than her mother, who was a large framed woman with glasses and blonde hair. If she could get the truth out of anyone, it would be Harry, she guessed.

As she sat down next to him, Harry sighed because she had that puzzled look in her eyes that he knew all too well.

"Beansie?" She asked.

"Oh yeah," Harry chuckled. "Well...that's what I've always called you...ever since you were about 2, I think. Your favourite food in the world was baked beans. Me and Mum could hardly get you to eat anything else, and "Beans" was your first word. It was a terrible year, I can tell you that now. You were already a smelly enough baby, but on a baked bean diet as well? Phew!"

Becca giggled. "I've actually had a craving for them for about 2 days now..."

"Noooooooooo!"

Becca laughed again.

After a slight pause, when all the laughter had quieted down, Becca's thoughts turned to something a little more serious. "I wish I could remember stuff like that. Well, everything. It might sound dumb but I start feeling really lonely sometimes. Usually at night. And I feel like the reason is not having those little memories to keep me company."

"Well, if I had the time, and if Mum hadn't have told me not to, I'd love to tell you everything about yourself."

"What? Why did Mum tell you not to?"

"Uh, just something that she said that the doctors said. Too much past information could scramble your brain up or something, for the future information."

"Sounds like baloney to me." Becca muttered. After a while she began twiddling her fingers, and turned bright red when she thought of something else she could cheekily ask.

"I'm sure if you told me just...one thing...my brain wouldn't get scrambled."
Harry looked at her suspiciously.

"What's with the girl that keeps mailing me?"
Harry said nothing but Becca knew he knew exactly what she was talking about. She continued, despite his non-responsiveness.

"No one will tell me anything, and she keeps sending me all this stuff...?"

Pulling a box from under her pillow, she poured the contents onto the bed. It was filled with letters, printed out emails, and tiny pieces of jewellery like bracelets and earrings.

"Uh..." Harry said, fidgeting uncomfortably. "A prank from one of your schoolmates or something maybe? How do you even know it's a girl, anyway?"

"The letters are too deep and emotional to be from any smelly boy. Plus, you must remember the incident in the hospital ages ago? I don't know, maybe I'm imagining it, but these letters..." She looked down at the beautiful handwriting on the letter between her fingers. "They seem...way too familiar."

She wrinkled her nose at the time she remembered seeing the girl face to face, that momentous day at the hospital. Why had the girl been so angry? It was something that frightened her a little, to think that there was someone out there who had such strong emotional feelings towards her, and she had no idea why. While she had been thinking about this, Harry had gone from being quite relaxed to very tense and alert. He was leaning forward with his fingers interlocked, rocking backwards

139

and forwards gently and staring into space. He loved Jasmine almost as much as Becca had once they had gotten to know each other all those years ago, and always remembered her full of love and laughter. It killed him to imagine her in the hospital now, and he felt like every word he uttered about her now was a betrayal, because he knew he would never be able to explain the whole story.

By order of Gina.

"D-do you think the letters are a trick?" She asked Harry, worriedly. "Do you think this girl is out to hurt me?"

"No." Harry said, quickly. He seemed surer about that than anything. "I promise you."

"Why can't you tell me about her, Harry?"

Becca looked at him, and her blue eyes pierced into him as she coaxed, "It's okay, y'know. You can tell me anything."

His eyes pleaded with Becca not to start prying into her past life, because he didn't know what his mum would do to him, if she found out that he was telling her things. At least, here and now wasn't such a good time, because the bedroom door was slowly opening. To save his sister's skin, he threw himself quickly into a sprawl on the bed to hide the letters.

"OH, Becca, you look <u>lovely!</u> But what are you two still doing up here? I've made porridge for you both downstairs, and it is getting ridiculously cold."

"We're just...finishing up, we were tidying the room." Becca smiled, a sickly sweet smile.

"Oh! Well good. You ALWAYS used to love tidying your room before the accident, sweetheart. I'm glad you're keeping it up."

Harry made the tiniest noise under his breath, laughing at the idea of Becca ever tidying anything before. It would have to be coming up to Christmas, or Becca's birthday for that kind of miracle.

"Did I like porridge before, Harry?"

He sat up when Becca addressed him, making sure the letters were still well hidden. His eyes were yelling a thousand things secretly to his sister, like: "Why are you bringing me into this? You want me to tell you more lies?"

Becca responded secretly with, "I just want to see what kind of things she wants you to lie about, and what she's okay with."

Gina suddenly interrupted their thoughts with an answer for Becca. "Of course you did, Becca! You loved it. Isn't that right, Harry?"

Harry lowered his head, surrendering to her. He muttered in a low tone, almost like a zombie, and as if it physically hurt him to make up such lies about his own sister.

"Yes. She loves porridge. Very much."

"Well then!" Gina blurted out happily, a huge grin on her face. "Get your skinny butt downstairs to eat it, young lady, and make sure you wash your bowl afterwards! Come on, Harry."

Harry was the first to get up after Gina flounced back downstairs. At the door, he threw a sad, apologetic look towards Becca, then closed it- leaving her feeling more confused and lost than ever before.

Chapter 14
Please come and take me home.

Jasmine looked at her reflection in the hospital's bathroom mirror and all she saw staring back at her was a disgusting shell of a person. A person that used to be beautiful. She stood in front of the mirror and raked a brush through her hair once or twice, then placed it down gently and stared into the mirror at her own empty green eyes.

Becca used to wish she could have my eyes, she thought to herself. I remember she always commented about them, and said they were pretty. Well...

"They will always be yours, Becca," She said aloud. "Because I will always be yours."

This long three months had almost killed her. She was sure that she had tried every treatment in any doctor's handbook, and while her hands healed up perfectly, the pain in her chest was getting increasingly worse and that was something they couldn't heal, so she had decided that now it was time to go home. She hated seeing Archie worry so much that he had lost weight from the stress of everything...staying up with her in the hospital almost every night and watching her spend hours crying into his arms.

When she wasn't daydreaming about the amazing history her and Becca had shared, she sat and hoped that her letters and presents were getting through to her. It numbed the feeling of uselessness, and it gave her hope that maybe in time she might remember and they could start again, despite Harry's warning. And Gina's warning. She had realised that the story about the incidents at the hospital was local news now, as while she had been resting just this morning, people had peered through her window just to snigger and laugh, not even bothering to hide their jests. Jasmine didn't really care about that. She knew that there was someone in the world who would care, and protect her from everything, if she could just remember. There was no law or restriction on earth that she felt could stop her from seeing Becca today and letting her know the truth that no one had been brave enough to tell her. But then suddenly she stopped, taking a moment to analyse the situation. A horrible pain in her stomach formed when she thought about the worst that could happen.

Maybe they had brainwashed her too much in the past months, and she'll just laugh at the feelings I tell her about tonight? Maybe she'll call the police herself and have me locked away forever?

No. That just wasn't her Becca, whatever had happened.

For one, tiny fleeting moment, a thought popped into her head that horrified her. *There's always an alternative*, the scary voice in the back of her head whispered. *There is always the girl from school, Anna, who is ready for you to become hers*. Anna? Jasmine shuddered when she remembered that awful first day at school where that confused, gothic, lesbian wannabe tried what she did with her. Or just as bad: that prediction her mother had for her, all those years ago. The generic picture of a husband and three fat grandchildren. This to any other person would have been fine, but it wasn't the life she wanted and she knew it.

145

Violently shaking her head, and it almost brought her to tears when she realised that these would be the worlds she would have if she gave up, but she silently vowed that they would never happen.

Archie popped his head around the bathroom door. "You ready?"

Jasmine sighed. She couldn't even remember if she even answered or not, but soon enough they were walking down the road side by side. People on all sides of the pavement and in their cars and shops were trying to burn holes into her with their judgmental, disapproving eyes. The stares were merciless, and Jasmine suddenly wasn't sure she was ready for all this yet. She hadn't expected it to be this harsh. "Easy," Archie coaxed, when he felt her hand tighten up inside his. Just when she felt like she was about to hyperventilate, the situation only got worse. In the middle of the square, Gina stood proudly handing out flyers with the biggest, most smug look on her face. Archie acted quickly and they changed course, going down a small alleyway instead of the main square so she wouldn't see them, and was about to walk that way instead when Jasmine protested.

"Let me just hear for a sec..?"
Her father shrugged.

"St. Mary's church is here for you twenty-four seven! Any problems you have, I want you to bring them to me, Vicar Jameson, tonight at eight. All in pain shall be healed! All sinful afflictions will be lifted with the power of God! Just look at my daughter Becca, who came back to us from the grasp of the Devil."

Jasmine made a face.

"Now I've seen god's servants before..." Archie chuckled. "...and they don't look like her, that's for sure."

"I know." Jasmine smiled. As they walked the remainder of the journey home, her brain had leapt into overtime. She realised that moment had worked out better than she had ever planned, and although she hated an audience, she knew where Becca would be for sure now, and that was something.

Chapter 15

Someday it will be all right... but not today.

"For thine is the kingdom, the power and the glory, for ever and ever, Amen."

"Amen," Becca muttered. She didn't bother to look up at her mother, who she reckoned was probably staring at her. She had been sitting here in church, twiddling her fingers and feeling terribly awkward. However, regardless of how she felt, she still believed what her mother had told her: that she had loved church before the accident, and attended every night. At this stage she hadn't yet had a reason not to trust her mother, and had been provided no other alternatives. She glanced up and saw her twin brother, standing with his electric guitar with four other boys, and they too looked bored and miserable, but when they caught her eye they responded with huge fake plastic smiles. Something was going on.

Meanwhile, Jasmine was running. She ran through all the small side roads in the dark, trying to escape extra attention. She knew nearly everyone in the neighbourhood was on Gina's side, which made it hard to do anything without spies reporting back, adults interfering or kids bullying her. Her breath came out in sharp, shallow breaths as she anticipated what she was about to do, but also remembered why she was doing it. All those years ago, a girl who practically had saved her from insignificance in school, pressed her lips against hers and told her that she loved her. Becca had built Jasmine up from the moment she'd met her, in confidence and strength, making her a better person. Now the tables had turned, and it was Jasmine's duty to save that person in almost the same way she had saved her. What better way to declare love than in a room crowded with disapproving people?

Becca's mother was about to launch into another long speech. Becca could just tell because now she had her serious face on, drawn out the Bible from the stand and was flicking through the pages squinting to find the right passage. But that was when she stopped dead in the middle of a word. Her eyes locked onto the glass doors at the back of the church, where something or someone hovered outside. Becca turned slowly to see, as did everyone else in the church. And then, when a girl was seen running almost full speed towards them, pretty much everyone except Harry and Becca gasped.

"Stop that girl!" Gina yelled frantically. "She is trouble, and I will not have her in my church!"

The Ushers had no chance of getting there in time because the girl was lightning fast, and seemingly on a mission. She pushed hard through the doors, and kept running. People jumped out of their seats and began yelling and shouting but Becca remained calm and the realisation dawned on her that she knew this girl. Harry was suddenly at Becca's side and while her mother began storming down the altar steps, she felt the girl grab her arm. She had decided against the big romantic speech as her more rational senses took over, and all she wanted to do was get Becca the hell out of there.

"Come with me, please," The girl said softly, over the commotion. "Now."

"What?" Becca said, confused.

"You have to go, they're going to catch you." Harry whispered quickly. "This isn't the time or place..."

"You know your mother won't let me get anywhere near your house! I cant take it anymore, she needs to know. Becca!"

Jasmine didn't have any time to finish what she had to say because like a shadow, a sense of darkness encased her and she knew Gina was right behind her. That was it. That was the amazing master plan finished, and Jasmine felt it crumble to pieces within her. She'd completely blown her chance. Gina grabbed her by her hair and began to drag her down the aisle back outside the church. As she screamed in pain, Becca was absolutely horrified as she watched, but no one else seemed to care or question it. *Why was everyone always on her mother's side? It was like she was the be-all-and-end-all in this town. Had it always been like this?* She wondered.

"Becca!" Jasmine screamed again, almost choking on her own tears as Gina tugged her harder.

"We do not accept troublesome, meddling adults like this in our church!" Gina shouted to the masses, as if parading her as an example as she cried.

"Get off me! I want Becca," She sobbed.

"Why does she want me?" She asked a stranger beside her, but the stranger simply moved away, ignoring her.

"She's crazy," Another woman said. "...And evil."

"I won't let them take you away, Becca. One day you'll know the truth. One day I'll tell you-"

Gina stopped dragging her then, and in pure rage, slapped her hard across the face.

No one said a word or even moved except Becca and Harry, who responded with mouths open in shock, as the sound of the slap resounded against the walls of the House of God. *Gina had never even slapped anyone before,* Harry thought to himself. *In Public...*

Jasmine was also so shocked she couldn't even cry anymore. A terrible red bruise began to blossom on her cheek, and as she stared at Gina, she hardly had time to respond before she was dragging her by the hair again.

"Get out!" Gina cried. "Get out of here, and don't you dare come back!"

Through the glass doors everyone watched Gina throw Jasmine out on the pavement, and saw her hit her arm on the floor as she fell. Yet again, no one said anything. The thing that stunned Becca the most, however, the thing that may haunt her forever was the fact that they continued the service after all that. Even Harry continued playing dull Christian songs on his guitar in obedience to his mother. When they eventually left, it was night time, and the girl had gone- as if she had never been there in the first place. Becca uttered not one word to her mother after that, and couldn't even look at her. As she got home she ran upstairs, and for at least two hours, she cried the most awful, bitter, unstoppable tears.

Chapter 16
"Not knowing" hurts too badly.

The dreamy, shocked feeling still hadn't escaped Becca as she jumped into the grey eight-seater van for work, when it came for her the morning after. Everything felt surreal and wrong to her, her work uniform felt itchy, and though the people were friendly at this new job, she felt alone.

She threw herself into a seat at the front and leaned her head against the window, quickly pulling out her MP3 player before the other people could call her to come and chat with them at the back. When she pressed play, classical music blazed through her headphones, and instinctively she made a face and pulled them out. Classical? Did I ever like classical? She didn't know what she expected but it wasn't the likes of Mozart.

The van turned a corner and passed into a new lovely neighbourhood, about two blocks away from her own. It still looked beautiful even when tiny droplets of rain started to hit the pavements, and gloomy grey rain clouds loomed above it. Still leaning against the glass, she suddenly felt the urge to look closer at the familiar landscape, because the closer the van pulled towards a certain house, the more curious she felt. She couldn't understand it, so she observed every inch of what she saw. The door was opening...and by some magical twist of fate, or a lucky coincidence...she came face to face with the ghost of her past. Yes! It was her! The girl that she'd seen at the church, and in the hospital. She was in her own world at the moment though, fiddling with her keys, and hadn't spotted Becca in the van. Becca whizzed round to double check as they rode on, shaking her head, to make sure she wasn't imagining it. Who was she? The mysterious girl she always saw in her dreams and in the shadows; with tanned skin, sleek black hair and murky green eyes?

"Stop!!" Becca shrieked, and jumped out of her seat. The van driver automatically hit the breaks, alarmed by the yell. "What's the matter, Becs? Forget something?"

"No, no! I mean-" Becca paused a second, and almost chuckled when she thought of the irony from that sentence, but she quickly ignored it. "Look, please, just let me off here. There's something I have to do, I'll catch up with you in a little while."

"Catch up?" The van driver said, shaking his head in bewilderment.

"Just let me off!" Becca screamed again. The driver clicked the door locks up and Becca ran out into the rain. Despite the cold raindrops, she only pulled her hood over her head to shield herself from the burning eyes of her work mates already gossiping and staring behind her, and as she began blushing, the heat from her face could have provided central heating for a house.

She ran as fast as she could back to where she'd seen the girl- and sure enough there she was, putting her keys into a small pouch bag. Becca had almost reached her when, frightened, the girl darted of down an alleyway. Her light feet swept past the pavement and the puddles like some graceful ballet dancer or athlete. "No, Stop! Wait!" She cried, hauling her heavy work backpack around her shoulders and following her. It seemed like no use, and Becca's heart sank. At the speed the girl had disappeared Becca felt like she'd lost her forever now. She stopped running and trenched forward miserably instead, wondering where she was and where she could get a taxi ride to her workplace...but then suddenly, in the rain, at the end of the alley, stood the mystery girl. She had stopped. Why? Becca had no idea but her heart leapt a little. There was just a small alleyway separating Becca and the girl who held all the secrets of her past. The girl stood very still, apart from her chest that heaved up and down heavily from the running, all tensed up as if she wanted to run away again. In the pouring rain now, Becca squinted to see the girl properly, hoping that it would bring some memories back, but she could not see that far. Gathering up all her courage, she yelled into the rain.

Who are you!?"

The girl said nothing, and did not move.
"What do you want from me?!"

The girl said nothing, and did not move.
"Why did you crash the church service like that yesterday?!"

Becca waited, and waited. Her cool breath came out as mist as she exhaled heavily into the air, and realised she was shaking a little. It isn't that cold, surely? Becca wondered. In her heart she knew it was only because she was both excited and scared. Her mobile phone felt like a dead weight in her pocket, and she wondered if this was such a great idea after all. Running into an alleyway, alone, after a girl who she only remembered as unstable and violent? Would she have time to call the police if it was necessary? She could not clearly see the girl's face from where she was, and so her emotions were a mystery. But then the girl suddenly fell to her knees. After a pause, Becca rushed to her thinking she might have been hurt- but when she got there she noticed the girl was simply distraught with sobs. "It's okay," She whispered, hugging the girl tight, and ignoring the raindrops pouring off both their faces. After a pause, she took authority of the situation, forgetting her fears. "Let's get you home."

She couldn't imagine what she had been worried about all this time. As soon as she touched the girl, she felt that the girl would never want to harm her, and she had the overwhelming urge to just make this girl feel better, whatever it took.

Chapter 17

It's taken forever to get back to this point.

Jasmine felt her heart beating so irregularly that she knew she was about to collapse when she heard Becca's voice again for the first time in three months. Her legs could not hold her up any longer. It was like all the strength that she'd been so bravely gathering up, just to do even the simplest tasks every day- simply dissolved into nothing, and she just wanted Becca to hold her again like she used to. She had only ran because, not seeing Becca's face at first, she expected it to be some dumb kids from the old school come to throw rocks at her or something like that. She had really expected the worst, but now she couldn't have wished for better.

It was almost surreal to Jasmine as Becca checked her over, then took her arm and flung it over her shoulder to help her up. "It's okay, let's get you home." She crooned. It was the most beautiful sound Jasmine had ever heard. Shakily, Jasmine opened the front door of her house and they went upstairs into Jasmine's bedroom. Becca could hear a man in the living room, chomping away on some noisy food and bellowing at the TV screen happily. Must be the football, she thought to herself. Becca helped Jasmine onto her bed, and even though they were both shaking from the cold, Becca was observing Jasmine's every move, like they were playing pretend doctors. "You should get that coat off...Jasmine." Becca tried her name out for size, hoping it would trigger something, and Jasmine shivered as she said it. After giving her a few more firm orders in her pretend-doctor tone, Becca then took her own bag and coat off and lay them down on a chair beside the bed; then sat down next to Jasmine, who still hadn't moved, and helped her with hers too.

"Y-You...seem...very at home here." Jasmine said, testing her, and fighting the cold as her coat was taken off.

"I feel at home at quite a few places. It's weird. But it's all part of my past life, the one I had before my accident. I don't know, maybe

161

I've been here before. I was wondering if you could help me with finding that out."

Becca put her elbow on the top of the chair and used her hand to support her face, then her eyes flashed the way they usually did when she was puzzled. She waited a while until they had both warmed up a little, in a comfortable silence, then she began the questioning.

"Who are you, really?" She blurted out. "And what do you have to do with me and my life? I'm sick of all the lies going on here, and being so confused all the time. I just want the truth and I don't care how bad it is."

After a pause, Jasmine replied with a whimper. "It's not bad, at all. I'm your girl. You and me used to be together. A real couple with past history and plans for a future. The car crash totally wrecked all of that for us. Nearly everyone in the neighbourhood has been hellbent on keeping that a secret from you, so that's probably why you've been a little confused, and I was in hospital so I couldn't have gotten this resolved as fast as I wanted to…"

"No!" Becca gasped. "That can't be true! I haven't...I mean-"

"Yes, I'm sure your mum has been filling your head with all kinds of stuff, but it wasn't the truth, this is, I swear. I have pictures of us from the very first year of high school, valentine's cards, letters, texts, emails, everything! Just name it and I'll show you whatever you want."

There was no suitable answer or response from Becca on that one.

"...Why has everyone been lying to me?"

There was no suitable answer or response from Jasmine on that one.

"Were you really with me the day I got hit?"

Jasmine paused for a while, staring hard at the floor. Squinting slightly, she cringed as the horrific images flew right back into her head. Eventually she said, "...All the way."

"I was with you when the car hit you. I called the ambulance. I came with you in the hospital van, and I stayed with you until your family came, then I was forced out...I was with you the moment you came out of unconsciousness and I was stabbed in the heart when you turned to me and asked me who I was. You couldn't remember me. You could remember your stupid family, your horrible bible-bashing mother but you couldn't remember me...? Jasmine? I thought you loved me. God, it hurt so much Becca. You will never understand what I've been through without you, we were so perfect together. I...I asked God every day, why me, was my sin so wrong, wasn't there any other people in the world that he could punish? Murderers or Pedophiles, maybe? but no. He chose a small town girl and took her love away from her. I've never felt anything as strong as what I feel for you. I've tried moving on alone but it just feels like there's no point at all. It's just you that I love, Becca. I love you so, damn, much."

Jasmine tried to calm herself down before continuing.

"Maybe it was all my fault. It was your birthday, and I knew you didn't want a big fuss but I really wanted to surprise you. I'd made a cake, I'd wrapped all the presents, and I just wanted to make it perfect. Everything just got so messed up. It was never meant to be like that at all. Becca, I would have never, ever wanted to hurt you, I swear. But it was all my fault. I almost killed you, and I'm sorry. God, I almost killed you!"

With that, she burst into tears. Becca looked at this strange, weeping girl. Her heart and soul had never longed for anyone else so badly, never wanted to just reach out and make her feel like everything was fine. Her brain was holding her frozen, however, as it tried to gather all the new information in her head. She'd just found out, if what Jasmine was saying to her was true, that she used to be a lesbian with a girlfriend, and was living a happy life with her. It was obviously not a mother's first choice for a daughter, but her fists clenched up when she realised how long her mother had kept this from her. Isn't this MY decision? She growled to herself. Wasn't it my right to know that I was hurting someone in this way without even realising?

Hesitantly, and very gently, she raised a hand to Jasmine's cheek.

"I-It's okay. Please don't cry, I hate it."

Jasmine moved her head slightly towards her touch, and tried to stop the sobs that made her shake and the tears that slid silently down her face. The touch shocked her, but she welcomed it. She looked into her eyes and saw the familiar puzzled look as Becca explored her face, and touched her wet black hair with questioning fingers. "I wish I could remember," She said, smiling sadly. Jasmine wished that too, and nodded sadly in agreement.

"Is that why my mum hates you? Because we used to be a...a couple?"

"I think so. Well, actually, yes. Definitely."

"God! But that means that...all this time I've been avoiding you; scared of you, even, for nothing. I'm so sorry. I could see that something was hurting you, too, that was the most awful thing but I was just going along with what I'd been told. Everyone's been telling me what to think, and what to do."

There was a pause. "That's how I really know you're not yourself. Forget about it."

"I'm really sorry my mum hit you that day, too. I really couldn't believe it, and it hurt me so much to see it happen."

"Not your fault. I know your mum is a little crazy but to do something like that in public was a bit out of character, even for your mum. Is she still on her pills?"

Becca blinked. "Pills? What are you talking about? What pills?"

"She's been on a whole concoction of things for about a year now. I think she went a bit off the rails since her and your dad broke up, and they are meant to keep her calm, or something like that."

"I absolutely had no idea. Wow. I...I don't know if she is taking them or not."
Jasmine could hardly bear watching this new Becca act so afraid and lost in the world, her eyes scanning for information, trying to remember so much. Slowly she bent down to kiss her shoulder. When she rose back up, she watched Becca's face questioning things again, and ideas flickering in her eyes. After a while Becca moved herself forward, raising her other hand to Jasmine's face, and then leaned forward boldly so she could try to kiss her. "Oh no, Becca..." She half-cried, half-laughed. That was way too much too soon for Jasmine and she shrunk back. Is this all she thinks I want? She thought to herself, and the idea made her feel sick. "I wasn't trying to start anything sex-

ual." She plucked Becca's hand away from her face and set it down into her lap, but seeing hurt and confusion in Becca's eyes, she scooted over a little closer to her, ready to explain.

"This is <u>so</u> hard for me, you must know that, but I don't want to rush things." She said quietly, squeezing Becca's hand. "I've waited this long. As much as I want to, it wouldn't be fair to you. Of course I want everything to go back to normal, as soon as possible, but if we do everything in fast forward just for my sake, I won't have the beautiful girl I had before who felt something for me."

She was about to tell Becca to go home, and that it was too soon, because she didn't want her to feel pressured into any situation. But Becca was a girl who loved life in the fast lane, and sensing the rejection, she spoke fast. "I do feel something for you, Jasmine. Something I can't even explain. I mean, it's crazy- I just met you. But I believe every word you say, I see in your eyes that it's all the truth. With all the stuff I don't know I need someone like you, someone that I can trust. I just...I want to get the feelings back for you that I had. It feels like being without you is the reason I've felt so lonely. Please, can we just try this?"

Jasmine breathed out heavily, and knew it would be just too hard to turn her away. She fought back more tears as she felt Becca's sweet breath on her jaw line. Her soft lips began kissing her neck and as they slowly began rising up to her lips, chills ran right up Jasmine's back even though she wasn't cold anymore. Jasmine's hand led itself into Becca's silky hair, and the other onto her waist as she kissed her back. Then, holding her face in her hands, she looked into Becca's steel blue eyes and wondered how she had survived for the past three months without her. "Do...you feel anything?" She said uncertainly, hoping the kiss might have triggered something. Becca looked down at the floor, wondering if she should lie, but in the end she smiled and muttered, "I'm feeling a lot of things right now." Her lips brushed down to Jasmine's neck again, and heard Jasmine moan quietly. She breathed in her floral perfume...and the sounds and scents were almost things that she felt she remembered. Still kissing her softly, and feeling a little more confident, she ran her hand slowly down Jasmine's shoulders, then down into her white blouse. After a bit of fumbling, Becca's hands began to feel numb with panic...and she fell silent, which would have been a rarity in her old life. She struggled to pull her eyes away from Jasmine's tiny frame, and eventually she managed to feel around until the first button popped open between her fingers. Jasmine didn't flinch or move away. Instead she sighed, dropped her hand slowly down to Becca's thigh, then manipulated their positions ever so slightly so the both of them were moving naturally, and effortlessly, onto her bed.

The rain continued trickling down the misty panes as the two lovers, old and new at the very same time, began to find each other again. The wind smashed on every rooftop loudly, scattering the raindrops in a thousand different directions, but they could not hear them. Jasmine's dad downstairs could still be heard laughing and yelling at the TV screen because his football team was now winning- and he felt like the luckiest and happiest person in the world. But his daughter would have definitely begged to differ as she held her perfect girl in her arms. She had no idea how long she stayed there with her, frozen still in what felt like a gap in time altogether...just watching the rain settle and the sun finally bow out of their show. Feeling the most contented she'd ever felt in her life, she allowed herself too, like Becca, to close her eyes...and drift happily off to sleep.

Chapter 18
A dream,
and a divorce.

Becca had no way of telling if her dreams were a way of connecting with her past, but she'd like to think so.

In this dream or memory, she was much younger and she saw herself in the kitchen of her house. She was not in a very good mood. Gina walked in, also not in a very good mood, but for a different reason.

"Your father's here." She announced, in a very matter-of-fact, militant tone.

Becca jumped up, and her bad mood disappeared for that split second, as her rugged and extremely huggable dad came through the door with his trademark smile. "You said you wouldn't be here 'til the weekend!"

"I figured the weekend was too far away. I missed you WAY too much, Beansie." He laughed in reply.

The laughter soon subsided when they both turned around and realised Gina was still standing awkwardly in the doorway. It seemed like her face had a permanent scowl whenever her dad, Shaun, was around. "I thought you were here to discuss the divorce settlements."

He sighed. "Yes, I will in a minute. But right now, Becca and I need to talk. Can we have a minute?"

"She has homework," Gina snapped.

"I'd like to know if my daughter's favourite meal is still chips, with chocolate cake for dessert. Me and Jenna would like to make it for her when she comes over to our new house."

Gina's teeth grinding together inside her mouth was almost audible enough for the whole neighbourhood to hear. Jenna was the new, younger replacement that Shaun had chosen over her, and she hated the very mention of her name. It was enough for her to bolt out of the room with steam coming out of her ears. Despite all that...the whole breaking up of family and all...Becca still loved her Dad more than anything.

"That was mean, Dad," Becca grinned.

"I know," He winked. "I really, really shouldn't have...she's in enough of a state as it is, but she brought it on herself. Now, are you going to tell me what is wrong?"

"How did you know something was wrong?"

"When I came in here, your face almost resembled...your mother's."
Becca laughed.

"...It's Jasmine."

"Go on."

"There's this school play coming up. Romeo and Juliet. Jasmine auditioned and got the part of Juliet, and this boy Nathan is going to be playing Romeo."

"Ah, I see."

"I wouldn't mind so much usually, in any normal situation...but this guy Nathan, he's a real jerk! I think he'll try something. I really don't like the idea of them rehearsing together alone...and don't even get me started about the kissing scene."

Shaun laughed deeply, and cupped her comparably smaller hand in his. "God, I hate being the one that has to break this to you, Becca. But, there's always going to be school plays. And chances are, Jasmine will always want to take part in them. It doesn't mean every boy is ready to steal her away from you because they steal a kiss on the stage!"

Becca pouted.

"You get this stubbornness from your mother. But maybe, the protectiveness from me." He smiled. "You're just going to trust me on this one, you can't hide her away for ever, and you have to trust that your love is strong enough. Do you want to know the most important thing?"

Becca nodded.

"Jasmine is head over heels for you. And that's why you, my girl, have nothing to worry about."

Chapter 19
The morning after

Jasmine stirred gently at first as Becca snuggled closer into her, but then her eyes snapped awake, and she realised that she had to wake her up now or they'd get way too comfortable and she would have to stay the night.

That would be a shame, the naughty part of her brain said sarcastically.

Shut up! We don't want to get her in any more trouble than she will be already with her crazy mother. We'd probably lose her forever then, the sensible part of her brain said in reply.

"Becca?" She whispered softly, then nudged her. Becca wrinkled up her nose, then yawned, making Jasmine giggle. "Are you okay?"

"...Yeah...thanks." Becca's voice was groggy and uncertain, but at least Jasmine didn't see any signs of regret from her for what they'd done. *She didn't wake up and run away screaming,* Jasmine thought, *so it looks like it's going well so far.*

"H-How are you?" Becca said quietly.

...WONDERFUL!! Jasmine's naughty voice replied.

Shut up you. Don't act too over eager, her sensible voice replied.

"I'm cool," She said calmly.

"I think I should probably get you home now. I mean, your work finished about two hours ago, so your mum will definitely be wondering where you are."

"Oh, I don't care." Becca said grumpily, folding her arms across her chest. "It's war between me and that woman now. I mean, she was trying to recreate another daughter, someone who wasn't the real me. What am I, a robot? How could she?"

Jasmine touched Becca's arm sympathetically to stop her getting too upset. It worked, and Becca exhaled a big breath of air before continuing. "Would the old Becca care about coming home late from work, or school?"

Jasmine snickered. "Never in a million years. Me and you used to go to the beach nearly every day after school, despite your mother hating me. We'd get ice creams, watch the birds, and just generally hang out. And sometimes when you were feeling adventurous, we'd even jump off the rocks for fun."

"No way!" Becca gasped.

"Yeah, of course! I was usually the scaredy-cat one out of the both of us, but you, you were always up for it. I even met you up there, around the first week of school. I was new in town but it had already gotten out that I was a lesbian, and everyone had teased me about it the whole day. I ran out as soon as the bell went and found my way up there, just to be alone. That's when you came along. I hadn't seen you in school, because you told me that you'd had a dentist appointment that day. But you said not to listen to them, and you said the next day you'd come in with me and we could hang out together. They never teased me anymore after that, ever. You were fierce and beautiful and strong, and everyone respected you whatever you did. So even when you told everyone that you and me were starting a relationship together, no one dared make any jokes. We were happy. Very, very happy. Up there on the rocks you told me that I should never let anyone make me ashamed of who I am, that I should never be ashamed of my decisions in life and never ashamed of what I wanted to do."

Becca smiled at the story. It seemed so unlike her now.

"...And then," Jasmine grinned. "A few days later, you grabbed my hand and made me jump off the cliff with you."

"What?! I never!" Becca said, after bursting out into giggles. "Now I'm an attempted murderer in your stories?"

"No of course not, but you know. It was a statement that we were going to get through hard things together."

"I see."

"It's hard trying to explain your old crazy theories to you...I mean, you're the one who made them, you're supposed to know!"

Jasmine laughed at her own comment, but soon after saying it she felt a ball form in her throat as if she was going to cry. It was supposed to be a happy conversation, but it just made her miss the old times.

"I'm not sure I can face my mum on my own." Becca then said, fidgeting uncomfortably and using the change in atmosphere to confess her true feelings. "I'd much rather stay here...with you...and hear about how I used to be."

Jasmine snorted. "No point. You know who you are deep down, and everything about your natural character will come back, I know it. The past is nothing now if I'm the only one that can remember it. Let's just focus on the future and making new memories, hmm?"

"Okay."

Becca looked into Jasmine's beautiful green eyes, suddenly blushing deep red. She fought through her embarrassment just enough to hoist herself upright on the bed, then leant over to peck Jasmine on her lips. It was the first time since she'd been back that she felt like there was no secrets- only friendship, safety and love between them.

"Tomorrow then," Jasmine said quickly, trying to hide her joy inside with a firm grown-up voice. "We'll go and tackle your Mum together. Okay? Do anything you can to avoid going to work; make her stay with you so you can start sorting things out, and then I'll come to help. Geez, I'm really scared too. But we can do it together...for sure."

Chapter 20

The nightmare began again.

The morning sun peeked through Becca's window like a tiny perverted boy spying on her with a telescope.

Usually she enjoyed feeling the warm summer rays on her face when she opened her eyes in the morning, but due to the things she'd found out yesterday everything seemed surreal and wrong...and she felt like everything would continue feeling like that until things got sorted. Luckily she hadn't had to deal with her mother last night. Jasmine dropped her off, donning an Indian sari around her face so no one saw them together, and Harry greeted her at the door with a huge smile.

"Mum's gonna be out at church until late." He said cheerfully.

She had a bite to eat, and went to bed...

Then BAM. It was morning, and the dreaded time had come.

She could already hear her mother downstairs singing and coaxing her downstairs for breakfast. She slipped on her fluffy pink bunny slippers and pink dressing gown, then slithered down the stairs like a cat burglar. She never took her eyes off her mother as she made breakfast, not even to say good morning to her brother; stepping around her warily and ignoring her chirpy voice preaching on about things like the weather and the morning paper. Eventually though she sat down and started on her soggy porridge, trying to decide in her head what to do.

"...and the postman is ALWAYS so late, it drives me mental." Her mother concluded. After a pause, she studied her daughter. "Are you okay, cherub?"

Becca winced. "I- uh..."

I don't want to talk to you. I want nothing to do with you, damn it. You're a liar and a horrible, controlling person: the voice in Becca's head said.

Her mouth, however, came up with something even more spiteful to say.

"I...don't...like...your porridge." She whispered.

"Excuse me?"

"I hate it, in fact. It SUCKS. I used to think that before, and I still do now. And you knew that, so why did you lie about it? You lying about something as small as that makes me wonder what else you've lied about."

Gina threw a deadly stare straight at Harry, which seemed to stop him in his tracks. Becca had never seen a deer in headlights like the well-known phrase says, but she imagined the look on Harry's face was exactly the interpretation of it at that moment. The doorbell rang then, releasing her magical hold on him, and he whimpered: "I didn't tell her anything." Before rushing out of the kitchen.

"Darling, what's made you think this? Maybe I put too much nutmeg in it this morning, that's all."

"Stop patronising me! You know this isn't about the damn breakfast...and I have memory loss, not brain damage. Stop pretending like we were close because I know we weren't! You must have been a real monster to me, because even memory loss couldn't get rid

the hatred I feel for you here, deep inside..."
She touched her chest softly, and for some reason a memory of her and Harry flooded into her head. Harry had awful scars on his back, but the only concern he had was holding her in his arms, telling her everything was all right, and trying to stop her from worrying so much about him.

"You're being silly now." Gina said, her face reddening with every word. "Of course we were...close. The best of friends, honestly. Who's been putting these silly things into your head? I mean, what would I have to lie about?"

"How about me?"

A small voice interrupted the two clashing titans, and they both whizzed round to see Jasmine standing timidly in the kitchen doorway. Harry, who had opened the door, now closed it quickly and scampered upstairs as if he felt like a bomb was about to go off. Jasmine threw an awkward grin at Becca, who winked back and smiled.

"What the hell are you doing in my house?" Becca's mum screamed.

"If you thought your petty threat would scare me away, w-well you thought wrong."

185

"Oh, my love." Gina said, chuckling. The laughter made more chills go up her spine than the anger she expected would have. They watched her hands slip across the kitchen counter, caressing all the objects, until her fingers came to rest on the largest kitchen knife she could find. "It wasn't a threat."

"Mum?" Becca whimpered as she saw the weapon in her hand, and Jasmine took the opportunity to run over and hide behind her.

"Y-You wouldn't dare touch me with that!" Jasmine yelled, but her eyes betrayed her fear.

"Wouldn't I? You're the one breaking restriction laws by being here, and after your little hospital incident, who would believe you? Would you like to be sectioned again? I'd call it self defence, and tell them it was you who burst into my house and tried to kill me." Gina laughed. "Maybe I'll cut your disgustingly long hair off first...it would make you look a bit like a boy at least...seen as you INSIST on trying to steal my daughter, and touch her with your, your...sinful hands."

She then turned to her daughter. "You found her again then, did you Becca? After all my hard work of trying to keep this filthy creature away from us?"

"How dare you-"

"Every-thing-was-going-so-perfect. And you've ruined it again, just like the first time. Why can't you just have been normal? All I wanted was a normal daughter who works hard at school, gets a boyfriend eventually and gives me grandchildren. That's how it's supposed to work."

"So people keep saying. Life was never going to work out exactly as you planned, mother. It doesn't for anyone. I'm sorry I couldn't be more perfect for you, but this is just how it is. I have feelings for Jasmine."

"You're too young to know what romantic feelings are. For crying out loud! You're still figuring out who you are, and you throw words around lightly. You're just confused, and if you had kept your head down into some more books..."

"Stop it." Jasmine said quietly, shaking her head, her eyes brimming with tears.

"...I think we need to get out of here, darling. Seriously. Find a nice new neighbourhood, where we can really start again. You'll feel so much better when you stop trying to rediscover stupid little distractions from your past."

Becca ignored her mother. She held her breath and slowly turned to look at Jasmine behind her for reassurance. She was wearing a bright yellow dress this morning, that billowed out at the bottom and was patterned with bright yellow sunflowers. The dress was the only thing happy about Jasmine now though, because sadness came off of her in waves. Her sleek black hair covered her face and her face hung low, just like Harry's in the presence of Gina, and her eyes were already tear-stained. Just then in the corner of her eye, she spotted Harry appear in the garden, behind Jasmine. His eyes were full of fear that his mother would spot him too, so he kept low and hoped to God that his psychic twin abilities would come to some use at this moment. He frantically flailed his arms to signal Becca to be quiet. Then he made up some strange gestures with his hands. *Phone? Hat? Car?* Becca thought to herself in bewilderment, shaking her head.

Her heart began pounding loudly as she realised this could be the deadliest game of charades she would ever play. Would her mum hurt her or Jasmine? She didn't know. She touched Jasmine's hair, pretending to play with it while Jasmine argued with Gina, both of them unknowing of the game between her and her brother.

Harry slapped his own head in frustration, then mimed out the words slower. After a little more thinking, Becca's heart leaped as she figured out the puzzle, and it was two simple words. *Called police.*

She had no idea what to do now, except for the simple fact that she had to keep her mother in the room, entertained, and with the knife in her hand. Her idea came when she looked down and realised that her and Jasmine were holding hands. In pretend shock she released herself almost violently, and Jasmine's eyes met with hers in complete bewilderment.

She could hope that Jasmine would forgive her eventually for what she was about to do.

"You know what? My mum might actually be right. I don't...I don't know what I'm doing here, with you." She said quietly, dropping her gaze in embarrassment. Gina relaxed her fingers under the kitchen knife and grinned, feeling her daughter's will crumble, thinking that she'd won with her ambitious speech.

"We shouldn't be like this. Maybe it would be better if I did start again."

"What are you talking about, Becca?" Jasmine said, mortified. "No! You can't say that. I've already had too many months without you, and it's enough to know that I never want to go through it again."

"Maybe you'll get a boyfriend if I leave, and you'd be happy."

"What? Becca, I'm happy with you! Don't do this, please, she's brainwashing you. I can't do this on my own. I won't let her take you away..."

Becca looked at the floor, disgusted with herself. It felt like her heart was being ripped out hearing Jasmine beg. Especially after everything they'd done together. Especially because she was only pretending... But she kept her head down and said nothing.

"It's not wrong, Becca. No one forced me to fall in love with you. No one told me I was going to find you. Maybe it's a weakness in me, because I've let it control my life...but it isn't wrong what we're doing. Remember? You told me never to be ashamed of who I am and what I wanted to do."

"I think it's time you got the hell out of my house." Gina sniffed. When she took a step forward, Jasmine grabbed Becca's hand quickly. "If you were serious about this and if you really wanted me to leave, you'd look me in the eyes and tell me. I know you would. The real Becca would. You owe me that at least."

"I can't." Becca said, and it was true, because her eyes would give the whole game away.

Where are these damn police! She thought angrily to herself. *Please don't let my mum hurt her...*

Gina grabbed Jasmine around the waist suddenly, and threw her over her shoulder, knife still in hand. Jasmine was kicking and screaming now like a toddler as Becca's mother began carrying her away, and the tears that never seemed to truly end began once again. Becca did not move once.

"You really can't even look at me, can you?!" Jasmine shrieked. "Please, Becca, you don't need them! Stay with me, please, god, don't leave me again! No!"

Suddenly there was a tremendous crash, and the front door smashed open. Four men in uniform stormed into the house, seemingly locked on to Gina who held the kitchen knife in her hand.

"You are under arrest," The first man said loudly, then continued reading out the rest of the riot act. Jasmine wriggled out of Gina's grasp and dashed back into Becca's arms, while her mother tried to lunge at her with the knife. "It's her! It's that little freak you want, not me! She's stealing my daughter! Get...off me!"

Becca was almost in tears herself now, not knowing if she was feeling sadness or anger. All her shaking hands wanted to do was reach to Jasmine and hide in her embrace. Somehow though, finally, she gathered up the courage to walk towards her mother as two of them restrained her.

"You know what, Gina. I hope they lock you up for good. I hope you rot where they're taking you now, so me and Jasmine can lead our lives far away from here and use all YOUR savings to do it."

"Becca," Jasmine tried to put a hand on her shoulder.

"No, I want her to hear it."

Gina didn't seem to be comprehending anything at this point, judging from the way she was breathing heavily, and her eyes were locked onto Jasmine as if she would lunge at her any chance she got. But suddenly she started to laugh.

Then she said the most horrifying thing Becca could imagine.

"Well I wish...I'd hit Jasmine good and proper the day I tried to with my car."

Jasmine's legs buckled from underneath her. She was surprised that she could stand after she heard it, albeit having to steady herself a little. Two of the police officers lost their professional appearances for a second, their mouths dropping open at the scandalousness of the scene in their usually quiet neighbourhood. The one who was free from restricting Gina was as quick as a mouse, whipping out her notebook and tiny voice recorder.

"What?" Becca said, dry-mouthed.

"I wanted to crush her skull into the ground. It was the only thing to do, to rid you from that disgusting creature. I just wanted it to stop, Becca, do you understand? You were always my favourite and I expected better of you, so much better. She had to die. Was it my fault you were wearing her wretched coat that day with the damn hood over your face? The one she always used to wear? Why did it have to be you on that very day in March? I saw your memory loss as God answering my prayers, but just in a different way. I had you back, just not the way I planned."

There was a deadly cold silence in the room when Gina stopped talking, and everyone was in a deep state of shock. Gina was the only one that seemed to be functioning, her spiteful and high-pitched giggles indicating that she had truly lost it after revealing such a burden onto other people's shoulders, and no longer having to hold her poise. Becca was the second one to finally come back into motion. As she slowly leaned herself against the counter, she whispered: "Please take her away now."

She waited until they had finally left with her mother, who now was the one doing the kicking and screaming, until she could finally breathe out a long breath of air and be certain the trouble was over. "Are you both okay, girls?" A police officer came over and asked softly. Becca nodded, smiling politely, until she took a look at Jasmine. She touched her cold hands and realised that at a dangerously steady rate, Jasmine's shaking was getting worse and worse. She looked as if she'd gone to somewhere else completely in her mind, and that worried Becca. She shook her roughly until a single tear slid down her cheek, and she started hyperventilating.

"Whoa, Jasmine. Jasmine!" Becca panicked, holding her tighter. She pressed her face close to hers and forced Jasmine to look at her. "Don't do this. It's okay, I promise. It's okay."

"Should I get an ambulance?" The small policewoman said, her voice shrill and annoying.

"No! She can get through this. It's nothing. Jasmine, look at me right now."
Jasmine's eyes finally steadied but Becca didn't release her grip from her waist. "This is nothing." She repeated. "You're alive, and you're safe, I promise. No one here is going to hurt you."
Jasmine seemed to murmur the words back to her as if they were registering in her mind.

"Talk to me, Jas."
A few minutes passed, but Becca could tell as Jasmine's heart rate starting returning to normal by the clammy hand she'd set upon her chest, and when she felt it she sighed deeply with relief.

"I'm here." Jasmine whispered.

Together they took a few moments to breathe, and remember that the worst of it was now over. The selfish part of Becca wished she could just shut down like Jasmine did too, and not have to deal with anything at all. But right now, there were police in her house and a twin brother to look after, and like always, that was a responsibility she had to take.

"You're both very clever to have kept her talking all this time." The policewoman said, gently, trying her best to raise the mood.

"Thank you," Becca said, smiling politely again.

She led Jasmine onto a chair slowly, without saying a word. Then, remembering that Harry was outside too, she reached up and felt along the top of the back door to get the key, and allowed Harry back into the kitchen.

"Aw, sis." He beamed, his cheeks reddening. "Thank god you understood my message! I heard everything from the window. I...I'm sorry."

"I just can't believe it. Thank God they can just take her away now, to somewhere she belongs. But how could she?"

Harry looked down at the floor bashfully. "I did kind of know that there was a slight chance she'd do something awful, because she wasn't on her pills. Last time she wasn't on them, she did this to me." Harry tilted the palm of his hand and presented his burn marks. "But nothing like this. I couldn't even imagine her doing something like this..." His eyes cautiously flicked over to Jasmine.

"Why didn't you tell me?" Becca said, but then frowned at the expression. She must have knew these things before, so she corrected herself in her mind. *Why didn't he <u>remind</u> me?*

"Didn't want to worry you. Before, we both knew she was breaking down over her and Dad's divorce. Y'know? In a way I don't really think her hatred was about you and Jasmine being together- or the whole lesbian thing at all- it's just that she had other issues crushing her and that was one way to take her frustration out. Like Dad used to say: Misery loves company. If she couldn't be happy, she didn't want you to be."

"You do know she'll go to jail for what she tried to do...to my girlfriend. Don't you?"

Harry smiled sadly. "You say that like I care. I'm more concerned about what she tried to do."

"You should have told me about all of this." Becca pouted.

"I didn't want her to hurt you, Becca. Or me. Try to understand."

Becca suddenly felt ashamed when she saw her brother's face drop and he seemed genuinely hurt by what she said. When she got closer though and tried to comfort him, he grabbed her and almost tickled her to death.

"Stop!" Becca laughed, gasping. "All right, all right, stop!"

Harry laughed too, but then remembered Jasmine was there and she still didn't look too good. Her face was pale and she was staring into space, hugging her arms tightly around herself. He walked over to the chair she was sitting on, and crouched down beside her.

"Hello Pipsqueak." He said softly, smiling. "You're okay now, y'know. There's nothing to worry about anymore."

Jasmine's eyes snapped to him.

"I really missed you, and I'm sorry for anything bad I said about you and Beansie, because you too really are an amazing couple."

Jasmine shuddered. "This is just all...too much. Right now. I'm sorry."

Becca stepped forward, and began frantically waving her arms. "Oh, Jas? Just so you know, that wasn't really me talking when I said all those horrible things. Honest. I had to keep Mum distracted. Harry signalled me in the garden and-"

"You know what, it's okay. It's cool, really," Jasmine said quickly, jumping out of the kitchen chair before Becca could touch her. "I have to go now."

As she stood up, she really wasn't sure what to do with herself, but she knew she had to get away from there. Could her world could get any more sadistic? First her girlfriend's mother- usually a collected member of society and a church leader- comes at her with the dark intention to end her life. And then, the very person she'd been through so much for- Becca, her love- comes out and tells her that she should get a boyfriend and be happy. Words like that, especially from Becca, would be the end of her one day. And even though Becca had just explained that it was all a diversion, it still would have to be a while before she wanted to hear anything else Becca had to say. She couldn't even look at her right now, let alone be touched by her, so she quickly avoided Becca's advances. "Must you betray me with a kiss, Judas?" - was a phrase that came to mind; one that she'd learnt in Religion early last year. And even though it wasn't a kiss in this case, it had the same effect. She just didn't want to be hurt anymore.

"Jasmine...?" Becca called out.

"I have to go!" She snapped. Tears flooded across Jasmine's face again as she fled out of their house, and when she shut the door the echoes rang all the way through Becca's heart.

Chapter 21

...And she doesn't ever want to be without her.

Becca looked at her brother as he looked around the room and fidgeted uncomfortably as usual. Becca had bolted for the door almost as Jasmine had closed it, but Harry grabbed her arm before she could follow her.

"What are you doing?"

"I don't think it's a good idea to go after her this soon," He said softly. "Give it time."

"But I don't want to," She whimpered.

"It's not about what you want to do, Becca. Didn't you see Jasmine? Looks like you hurt her real bad. Nice one."

"Hey, I saved both of us! It's all your fault anyway!"

"I didn't tell you to make up the whole break up story." He shrugged.

Becca pouted, feeling her face redden up like a traffic light. "Well I'm going to go and sort it. I think me and Jasmine have been away from each other long enough, don't you?"

She didn't wait for a reply. Instead, she grabbed a wad of cash from the emergency pot in the living room, and called over the first taxi she saw when she got outside. Harry didn't stop her either, and instead he found himself standing at the doorway and smiling a little. "There's the old Becca I know and love," he muttered. He felt like some of her old qualities, like being stubborn as hell for instance, were finally returning to normal, and he had missed her.

Becca asked the taxi driver to wait for her when they pulled up at Jasmine's house, just in case she wasn't there. She ran up to the door and knocked on it loudly, but then realised she had no idea what she would say to Jasmine when they finally came together again. She ran a clammy hand through her hair and began breathing heavily, trying to remember what she would usually do in a situation like this, but she couldn't. Has this ever even happened before? She wondered. She was determined to hold her ground though, no matter how scared she felt. She sucked in a deep breath of air when the door slowly opened, and then the air gushed out of her lungs in disappointment or relief when it wasn't Jasmine. It was a tanned man, handsome in face with Jasmine's green eyes...but with the beginnings of a podgy beer stomach. To Becca's confusion the man's eyes opened wide, along with his mouth, and he blurted out her name.

"Becca!" He bellowed. "It feels like a lifetime!"

She raised an eyebrow. "Yep, it definitely does..."

"Good lord." He repeated, shaking his head. "I thought I'd never see you again. You don't remember me? It's Jasmine's dad, Archie! Have you seen Jasmine yet? She'll be mighty happy you came over. If I didn't know any better, I'd say you were the only thing that makes that girl happy. Lord knows I've tried without you here over these past months."

Becca blushed furiously at that fact, and almost forgot what she was doing there. She longed to go inside and hear more of what Jasmine said about her, but she struggled through it, keeping focused and ignored her childish vanity. "Is she here, Mr. Archie, sir?"

"Wow...'sir'? They must have fit some new programmes into your brain at that hospital. Never trusted them myself... It's just Archie. But no, I'm afraid not, sweetheart. Haven't seen her since this morning."

Becca suddenly got the most horrible feeling in the pit of her stomach. *If she wasn't here, then where would she be? She wouldn't do anything silly would she?* Becca didn't need her memory back to have noticed that Jasmine was as fragile as a water lily...someone who really absorbed misery and took even the smallest things to heart.

She thanked Archie, and when he closed the front door she marched miserably back to the taxi. "Could you just, er...just drive me around town, please," She said, knowing it must have sounded silly. The taxi driver shrugged, either not caring what her reasons were, or just not bothering to ask incase it made her more upset than she was already. Leaning against the car window, she desperately scanned her brain for any clues at all as to where her girlfriend would be. Her heart ached and silently cried out in a way Becca had never felt before, and she furiously choked back tears. *Ugh, this is stupid!* She said silently in frustration, furiously drying her eyes. I have to find her, I have to make this right.

The landscape whizzed past the window and at first Becca scrutinised it every step of the way. It was a warm and beautiful afternoon, and many children were out greeting and playing with the sun as it rose higher, singing to them from behind the clouds. People she couldn't remember stopped to wave at her, and politely but awkwardly she waved back, pretending everything was fine. After a while though her emotions got the better of her, and the objects outside the moving car became nothing but useless blurry shapes. Becca figured that she didn't need to look out so closely for Jasmine anyway. They had become so close in such a short space of time, she reckoned that she would feel Jasmine when it turned out she was near. She was so beautiful in Becca's mind that she envisioned her standing in the middle of the street- the only clear vision in bright colour- and she believed that her eyes wouldn't dare enough to look at anything else. At the moment her eyes were red and puffy. She closed them and breathed in deeply a few times to calm herself, which was becoming a habit for her, but then she did something that she was certain she'd never done before. She looked up into the sky, searching for a sign from her fairy godmother, or Abraham Lincoln, or whoever else was watching out for her up there above the stars and she whispered: "Please, please let me find her."

"What's that miss?" The taxi driver said then suddenly, making Becca jump.

"Oh...Nothing, sorry." She replied quietly. It was a good thing then that she had her eyes on the road, because as they turned the next corner she had that lucky, instinctual feeling again. "Do you think you could let me off here, actually?"

"No problem." The taxi driver grunted.

They turned into a car park and after paying the patient driver, Becca began to run...she had no idea where of course, but she just let her feet carry her to wherever they wanted to. Her heart leapt a little as she hoped her run was a very well known path from her past and she'd find her love nearby. She ran up a long flight of stony steps leading up to a cliff top until eventually, when she'd slowed to a slow jog, she realised she was at the seaside. She was on a wide rocky ledge, peacefully over-looking the sea- a spot only photographers would notice and realise the potential. Becca could see that maybe at one time in the past it was full here, because there were a few picnic tables scattered around and a rusty, abandoned ice cream van. But now, it was quiet there...and Becca was all alone...

...except for one person in a bright yellow dress, who was sitting on the ground clutching her knees tight with her hands.

She fought back tears and almost crumbled-like Jasmine had in the alley- as relief swept over her just by seeing that Jasmine was all right. However, she fought through it and managed to hold herself together. She had a duty to be the strong one, and she didn't want Jasmine to get any more worried or hurt than she already was.
She stepped forward with a new game-face on, and she was ready to keep her word: she would always be there to make Jasmine happy, what-ever it took.

"All right, who was it?" Becca shouted, storming forward and startling Jasmine. "Which loser in this world upset my Jasmine? I'll tear them limb from limb I will!"

After the initial shock, Jasmine burst into giggles. Becca came and sat down beside her, mimicking her posture and watched the sea waves roll in and out below. The laughter and few happy seconds soon faded away and they relapsed back into silence.

"...What were you thinking, Jasmine? Hmm? You scared me half to death, running away like that." Becca said quietly.

"Sorry. I was just a little freaked out. Your mother did try to kill me, y'know. And you told me you didn't want to be with me anymore. It just feels like whatever I do you keep trying to push me away again, so maybe subconsciously you really do want me away from you. You remembered so much stuff, so many people, from important to insignificant, but not me."

"That's the craziest thing I ever heard!" She protested. "You really think I had time to pick and choose people to remember while I was...y'know? Come on, Jasmine...Harry told me my hip had been broken in thirteen places. I think I had more important things to think about than trying to erase you. Honest to God, losing you again is the last thing I'd ever want to do."

"I can't do it anymore, Becs."

"Can't do what? Can't love me anymore?" Becca grinned, poking her. "That's not something you can switch off so easily."

"No, I mean...I just can't even try to make this work anymore."

"Well that's okay. You don't have to, that's why I'm here. You've done so much to get our relationship this far, and I'm so proud of you for that. No one's ever...well, for as long as I can remember-"

"Don't kill the moment," Jasmine smirked.

"Okay, sorry. No one's ever cared so much about me. And I'll never forget it. Just give me a chance to take the reins for a while, hmm? Repay the favour."

Jasmine didn't say anything for the longest time. They both sat there, looking out at the sun as it brushed beautiful pink and purple hues across the sky as it set. Then suddenly, in a burst of every emotion in the book, words billowed out from Becca that she didn't even believe she could muster.

"For God's sake, Jasmine!" she cried. "I can't do this with you. It doesn't feel right. Nothing about this feels in any way normal! We're not meant to fight, we're meant to be together...I don't have to have my memory to feel that. And God, if I can't be with you I feel like I might as well just throw myself off the rocks now! Please, Jasmine..." Only when the warm tears spilled down her cheeks did she realise she was crying. "How am I supposed to face them without you?"

Jasmine's face still seemed to be set in stone, until finally she slumped and dropped her defences, her eyes warm and sympathetic.

"Okay, Becca. I'm sorry, and I forgive you. Of course I do. Let's just forget it. That's something you're good at."

Becca tried for a laugh, but the tears were still marking streaks down her face. She took a few moments to compose herself, turning her face away in embarrassment. Then in an attempt to redeem herself, she made a crazy, offbeat comment.

"Why don't we jump off together?"

Jasmine smiled, in a reminiscent kind of way.
"That's something the old Becca would say."
"Well I'm sure she's still in me somewhere.
Come on, I'd like to give it a go."

Jasmine laughed. It was a beautiful sound,
comparable to Japanese wind chimes on a cool
breeze.
"Sure," She grinned.

* * * *

The cold water was the first shock Becca had
to deal with as she hit the water. She coughed
and spluttered, but when she eventually got
used to it she then let herself be immersed in
the cold foamy waves. It was peaceful and
beautiful at first, but then suddenly, Becca felt
a painful stab to her head as if she'd hit a rock.
She searched around but she couldn't see anything under the surface that may have flew up
and struck her. It hit her again, and the pain
was so searing and intense that she had to let
go of the breath she was holding and sunk un-

der the water for a few moments. Her head was pounding because as well as water all around her, images and sounds were flooding into her. It was fast and painful, but Becca laughed, sending bubbles from her mouth billowing up to the surface. She was returning. The pictures became more clear in her mind, and they began to make sense. A memory?

Me and Jasmine last Christmas. At Archie's, of course. She bought me a black hat to match her pink one, but I liked her pink one so much more that we swapped.

Becca gasped as she relived the scene all over again, and she couldn't believe her luck. She could hear voices everywhere, laughter and screams, bouncing off the waves in the water from thousands of memories that had past. A whole two years worth of jumping off the same rock, with someone she spent every waking moment with. If there was anything in the world that she was sure she'd never forget, it would have to be this moment beneath the waves, where both Becca's finally rejoined on that cloudy summer afternoon. Her memories were slowly returning. She knew then that it must have taken such a familiar shock to the system to trigger the beautiful reminders.

"Jasmine!" Becca gasped as her head bobbed to the surface, but her voice was hardly audible as the salty water rushed in and out of her mouth. She flailed around in circles, searching the rocks until she spotted Jasmine on the beach already, lying flat on her back, on the sand.

She swam to the shore with the hugest smile on her face. As she clambered out of the water, she knelt beside Jasmine's body, and even though she had her eyes closed, Becca told her the whole story.

Jasmine didn't smile. She didn't even open her eyes.

That was the moment when Becca's smile faded and she looked closer at Jasmine. She was as pale as a sheet and her once peaceful and beautiful face now seemed a little too, terrifyingly peaceful.

"Jasmine...?" Becca said, laughing nervously in case it was a joke.

When there was silence, Becca felt like she couldn't breathe. She was hyperventilating, and in a panic she roughly shook her. "Jasmine!"

Tears stung her eyes as she shook her and nothing happened. She was shaking hard, from the cold water on her skin and from the horrifying situation she was in, but she managed to bring one up to Jasmine's face.

"Jasmine, wake up. Please! Look, I remember you." She whispered, dropping tears onto Jasmine's wet clothes. "I remember everything. You are my everything. Don't you dare leave me now, when I've just got you back."

Once again there was no answer, or hint of reply. A loud gasp of air escaped from Becca's lips and then she began to scream. It was a woeful sound, chilling...like the sound of a thousand year old ghost still searching the waves for her lost love. Becca didn't have the strength to leave Jasmine to call for help, but she screamed until her lungs were raw and still she could not stop.

It was a peculiar sight. The people above were too high up to hear the screams, but they observed a small girl, cradling another in her arms, and kicking the sand as if it was the beach's fault for this tragic loss. Grey clouds began to roll in from the North, although the sea remained calm. And the two girls stayed there, together, but so alone at the same time.

Chapter 22
Rochelle

...Becca?

Becca? where are you?

Jasmine opened her eyes and squinted because of the bright light. Where she had just been on the beach, it was dark and gloomy. But here there was the kind of bright sunshine that usually comes after rain. To her amazement and disbelief, she realised that she was back outside her old school, in her old town. This was way before she had met Becca, back in the days when her world was hardly worth living, and she had been under the thumb of an athletic, blonde, vindictive and controlling ex girlfriend.

Rochelle.

She saw herself as she was over 3 years ago. Scared, weak, and sitting on a fence waiting for

Rochelle to come out of cheerleading practice. Dutiful: like a little lapdog. Rochelle walked out of the gym in her trademark way...like a supermodel off the television, always wearing sunglasses even when it was cold and wet, and always with her hair in vibrant curls that she flung around dramatically as she walked. As she saw Jasmine she smiled briefly, then threw her gym bag over for her to catch.

"Cheerleading really takes it out of me on days like this," - was the first thing she said. "I can't wait to get to my house and have some lunch. You really have to remind me about cutting the keys for you, Jasmine. I can get someone else to carry my bags, but I really need you to help me catch up with English class. Homework doesn't do itself! You could have totally had it done by now if you had the keys."

As she trotted along in front of Jasmine after saying that, something snapped in Jasmine's brain. So much so that she dropped Rochelle's bag on the floor, into a puddle on the road.

"Hey! What the hell, Jasmine? I have all my stuff in there! Pick it up!"

"I don't want to be with you anymore, Rochelle. I can't do it anymore."

"Don't be silly. Just pick my bag up and-"

"No! I'm sick of it. There must be someone out there better for me, who isn't going to treat me like this, and I'd rather wait for that person for sixty years than be with you now!"

Rochelle's mouth melodramatically dropped open. "Are you serious? You're dumping me?"

Jasmine paused for a second, terrified. If she said yes, who knows what a psycho cheerleader would do to her on a lonely street like this? If she said no, she'd be trapped with her forever, because she knew she could never conjure up this kind of anger and passion again. Rochelle would have broken her. She proceeded onto these next few steps very carefully, so not to anger the beast. "I don't even think...you really have feelings for me anyway. I see the way you still look at the boys at school, and I've heard all the rumours about you and them behind my back. You just want someone tread all over, and to do what you want them to, and I was just the loser who went along with that."

Rochelle thought about everything for a second, not particularly upset by what Jasmine was saying, just deciding what to do next. "Okay. If that's how you feel, then fine. I can always get Richard to do my homework and carry my bags. And you were right. Of course I didn't have feelings for you."

Jasmine's stomach tightened in agony from her words. Enjoying the reaction, Rochelle walked closer to whisper the rest of how she felt, hoping it would ruin Jasmine forever.

"Every moment I had to pretend to like you was like chalk down a blackboard. Kissing you was the worst experience of my life! You're pathetic, and a freak...but I gave you a chance, and now you throw it back in my face like this? Who in their right mind will ever want to be with you? Get it in your thick head: You're nothing. No one would even care if you died."

Why am I here? Why am I having this memory? Jasmine asked herself, watching the scene unfold. It still hurts as much as the first time.

"People would care if I died!" She screamed out to them, even though she knew it was just a memory and they couldn't hear. "There's only one person that matters! My Becca. I know she would care."

She spun around and looked up at the sky, turning her back on her old self and the horrible memory.

Becca! Where are you?

I don't want to be here. I don't want to see this memory. I want to continue my life, with Becca.

Becca!

Becca jumped as she heard her name being called. It was so soft she thought she might have imagined it...but then she lifted her head up from Jasmine's chest where she had been laid, sobbing, and saw Jasmine's lips mouthing the word.

"Jasmine?!" She gasped, and in a flurry of excitement and relief, she thudded Jasmine's chest until she gushed up water and coughed it all out. She cursed thankfully in her hoarse voice, flinging her arms over her and sobbing into her wet clothes.

"Jasmine...Oh, god, what happened? I thought you were dead!"

Jasmine's eyes flickered open, and she silently thanked the Gods for returning her to the beach that afternoon, to Becca's forlorn but beautiful face. She tried talking again but her voice and her vision hadn't yet caught up with her whirlwind of thoughts and emotions. Instead, she lifted a heavy arm and brushed strands of hair from Becca's face, willing her to stop crying.

"I remember it all now, Jasmine," Becca suddenly said, lifting her head up again. "Everything there is to remember, and it's all because of you. But then...I almost let you slip away. What would memories be worth if they cost your life? How could we have been so stupid?"

Jasmine only responded with her eyes, but they were full of fear and confusion. She wasn't at all sure if she'd heard correctly. Did Becca really just say she *remembered*? If this was a trick, it was an extremely cruel one.

While Becca pressed her cold nose onto her warm cheeks, she closed her eyes, wishing her words forward.

"I don't believe you." She said, then smiled sadly. She knew Becca probably thought it would make her feel better to pretend for just a few short moments, but if it wasn't for real then there was no point.

"What do you mean? You have to believe me."

"How can I, Becca?"

There was a rumbling from the past storm in the distance - as if even God himself was frustrated with the situation for a few moments. But eventually, something clicked inside Jasmine's head and she knew exactly what to say to resolve the situation.

"...Y-You know, your team lost the match this week."

Becca stopped, puzzled. Though after taking this thought in, she almost growled. "Those jerks!"

Jasmine shrieked, laughed, then jumped up to hug her. She knew then that it really was all over, and it definitely was her girlfriend of two years right there on the beach with her, as if she'd never been gone at all.

"I told you!" Becca laughed. "I promise you, all the trouble is over now. It doesn't matter that I remember the past, let's just concentrate on our new future. Jasmine Grant...will you marry me?"

Jasmine gasped. She almost fell right back into the netherworld from the shock of Becca's words. But before she could even answer, Becca had raced onto another subject.

"Let's get out of here."

"Oh...ok. Yes. The sand is soaking right through my shorts."

"No! I mean, let's get out of this town. We'll take Harry and Archie of course, but we're getting out of here, Jas. I mean it. I want to start again with you. You do want to marry me, right?"

"Yes, Becca. I absolutely accept."

"Let's stop talking about it then, and let's just do it."

"Where would we go?"

"Anywhere, Jas. Look, stop talking about it!" Becca laughed. She pulled Jasmine's head towards her and kissed her on the forehead, then jumped up and began walking away.

224

"Just imagine it! No more working in that awful diner!" She called back. "You could become a nurse, like you've always wanted! I'm just gonna start walking this way...and I want you to come with me."

Jasmine flopped back onto the sand for a moment, dazed and drugged with happiness. But then as soon as she'd caught her breath, she was back running after Becca again, a habit she soon realised that she'd never stop performing. "So we're just gonna walk the length of the beach together?" she said, once she'd reached her.

"Yes! Then from there, who knows?"

Gina Marie Jameson

Pleaded <u>Guilty</u> to Attempted Murder
on August 14th.

She was convicted and sentenced to 10 years,
but may be released earlier...

(leaving room for a sequel.)

About This Novel

This novel came about on my school's English Literature field trip, because something had to be done about the mind-numbing boredom of the lecture..! I noticed a girl in front of me who particularly sparked my interest, and I actually started wondering if I knew her, or where I'd seen her before. The bag that was draped over the back of her chair proudly displayed the name tag, "Becca". She had mousy brown hair and blue eyes, just as Becca does in the novel.

It's a creepy but useful thing writers do, observing someone and trying to come up with their whole life story, but it came to me fairly easily. I'd never written anything lesbian related before, but somehow I just couldn't imagine Becca with a boy...even after toying with the idea of Nathan instead of Jasmine as the main character. I thought it would be a really good chance to focus on the emotions of the situation and their love for each other, rather than a typical teenage novel that concentrated on the more lascivious feelings in the story. I believe that girls convey strong emotions with everything they think, say and do, and so I hope that having the two main female characters has provided a more evocative read.

Stephanie Lennox
Biography

Stephanie Lennox has written over 160 stories, plays and poems so far throughout her time as a writer. As well as winning the National *Get-Connected* competition in 2009, she won the *Vfifty* Award this year for this novel. Stephanie is also an editor for the teenage girl's E-zine, *Mookychick*, and a corporate sponsor of *NCLR*. She is currently living in London with her boyfriend, and this is her debut novel.

For More Information

Visit Stephanie's Official Website at:

www.stephanielennox.com

Made in the USA
Lexington, KY
25 October 2011